UGARIT:

TALES FROM A LOST CITY

J. TAMAREN

HISTORIUM PRESS U.S.A.

This book is a fictional narrative based on historical sources.

The names of the main actors are vouched for in the most authentic documents available to us: the clay tablets that were archived in ancient Ugarit and then baked in the fiery cataclysm that destroyed the city in 1190 BC. When the ruins of Ugarit were discovered in 1928 and the clay tablets were deciphered, they revealed a multicultural, sophisticated civilization about which we had known nothing. Characters other than King Ammurabi and Supilliulama and the merchant Urtenu are fictional. See the "Sources" chapter at end of book for other historical and literary sources that provided further inspiration for the book.

Library of Congress Registration Number on file

DELUXE EDITION HARDCOVER: 978-1-964700-32-8
HARDCOVER ISBN: 978-1-964700-33-5
PAPERBACK ISBN: 978-1-964700-34-2
EBOOK ISBN: 978-1-964700-35-9

Published by Historium Press 2025

To my friend Patricia Madsen: Thanks for giving me access to your library of books devoted to the ancient Near East. And for being my first reader.

Thanks to my grown children for their thoughtful feedback on early chapters,

and to my grandchildren for their existence.

CONTENTS

SPRING 1190 BC

More than three thousand years ago, Ugarit was a thriving city of trade along the Mediterranean coast. Ships arrived daily at its harbor, bringing valuable cargoes from Egypt, Cyprus, and the Mycenean-Greek city states. Caravans arrived from the Tigris-Euphrates valley, Arabia, and far-off Afghanistan.

The Hittites – a fierce empire to the north, in what is modern day Turkey – had won control of Ugarit as a vassal kingdom some 80 years before. They provided military protection to the wealthy sea-port, in exchange for tribute – gold, silver, precious cloths. And for a treaty of mutual support.

Egypt was the other mighty empire in the Mediterranean basin. The two empires – Hittite and Egyptian – provided peace to the region. Trade grew; cities grew. Couriers brought letters from one king to another. Scribes recorded trade deals, epics, and prayers. The palaces in the region were splendid, the temples richly furnished. Life was good.

Meanwhile, in the countries to the north of the Mediterranean---what we now call the Black Sea and the Balkans –and perhaps in the islands of the Aegean as well -- wars, drought, and famine were wreaking havoc. Thousands of people were leaving their homelands and heading south, searching for fertile land. The newly made emigrants traveled by land or by ship into the Aegean and ultimately the Mediterranean Sea. They became raiders, like the Vikings who ravaged Europe two thousand years later: engineering lightning quick attacks on wealthy cities that gave their targets no time to raise a defense.

Ugarit and scores of other seaports along the eastern Mediterranean did not know that a great storm was approaching.

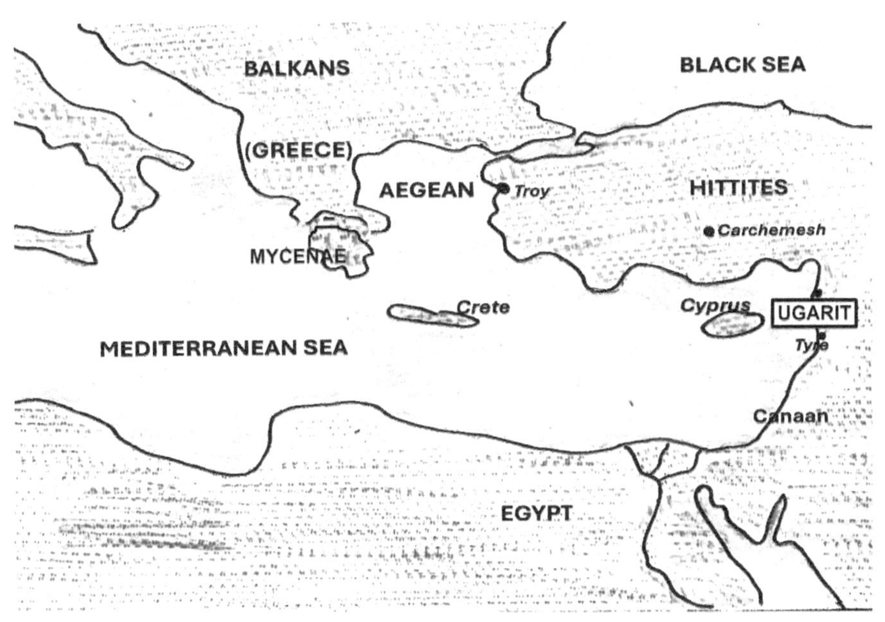

MAP OF EASTERN MEDITERRANEAN

IN THE LATE BRONZE AGE

Hittites: Their empire was centered inland, in what is modern-day Turkey, with control of some seaports along the Aegean

Mycenean-Greeks: Included multiple city-states on the mainland of present-day Greece and on nearby islands.

Balkans: A mountainous area north of Greece. The region now comprises Bulgaria, Croatia, and parts of Greece and Romania.

Canaan: In ancient times, Canaanites occupied parts of what is today Syria, Lebanon, Israel, and Jordan. Never organized into a single political entity, they were independent city-states that shared a common language and culture. Ugarit lay at the northmost margin of Canaan.

PART 1: A THRIVING CITY
EARLY SPRING

The gods helped build the Temple in the city. They provisioned the storehouse with wheat; they furnished the city with dwellings and building plots. They fed its people superb food. They gave its people superb water to drink. The Temple Courtyard was joyful with celebrants, the people sitting down on festival grounds, acquaintances eating together. They had monkeys, huge elephants, water buffaloes, beasts of faraway places, jostling each other in the wide streets.

--Adapted from "Curse of Akkad," a lament for a city destroyed around 2000 BC. See Coogan, 2013.

CHAPTER 1: ATTACK ON THE SUN

At the Healer's House

It was early morning at the house on Palace Street. In Yoninah's workroom, sunlight from the window slits fell onto her tables and shelves.

Yoninah enjoyed this time of day, the quiet time before any clients appeared. She was a healer in the lower city. Her clientele were the sailors wanting ginger to protect against sea sickness or amulets to protect them from the hazards of crossing the Great Sea. And the dockworkers from the harbor, who had aches and pains from lifting heavy storage jars full of grain or ingots of copper. She also saw the young girls seeking love potions to snare a lover, as well as the older women seeking to prevent another pregnancy when they already had several children.

Frequently, Yoninah's clients would be prostitutes. The women of the night would often have a child or two and would be seeking a way to prevent another pregnancy. Yoninah was invariably kind to these unfortunate women. The black-haired ones, the ones from Ugarit, had been abandoned by a husband and left to fend for themselves and their children. The yellow-haired ones, the ones from the Caucasus, had been taken as booty in war and sold as slaves in Ugarit.

Yoninah was a handsome woman in her early thirties. She wore a fine wool tunic, with a bronze pin at one shoulder. Her hair fell in a jumble of soft black waves, setting off her light brown eyes. She was young enough to be sympathetic to the young lovelorn girls and old enough to understand the plight of the women struggling to raise children.

Yoninah arranged her potions and shelves in their jars on her shelves. Then she ground up fresh Valerian roots, for the sleeping draughts her clients invariably sought. She said a quiet prayer to Asherah. A bronze figure of the Goddess stood on a pedestal near her shelves: "Queen of Heaven, give me strength to face the coming day. Give me wisdom in dealing with my clients. Give me patience with those who try my patience."

Yoninah also prayed to her loved ones in the afterlife: her mother who had taught her the skills of the healer and to her husband who had sheltered her and loved her for the years of their marriage. Her mother had died the year before, her husband five years past. She wished each of them a peaceful sojourn in the hereafter and assured them of her ongoing love.

As she paused for a moment in her work, she heard her daughters call out from the courtyard adjacent to her workroom.

"Mother, come see the birds!"

When she joined them in the courtyard, she saw a wondrous sight: thousands of birds filling the sky. Yoninah knew, from the years she had lived in Ugarit, that this was the time for their annual migration. They would have followed the Great Rift Valley, a fissure in the earth, that led from their winter homes in Africa all the way to their summer homes in the Aegean. Myriads of doves in formation, their gray wings catching the sun, provided a delightful display.

Her daughters Bat-El and Laylah were admiring the blanket of birds passing overhead. Bat-El, at age ten, was enthralled by the overhead display. She had the light brown eyes and curly black hair of the family. Her older sister, Laylah, was equally beguiled. She was fifteen, with the same black hair and brown eyes. She already had the curvaceous figure of their mother.

Then something odd happened. The sunshine dimmed. It seemed a cloud had passed over the sun, but the sky was cloudless. The cheeping of the birds decreased a notch as the cacophony became more muted. And the morning became darker. The day felt like late afternoon. The birds grew quiet and stopped flying. They settled on trees all over the city.

"The sun is going away!" Bat-El pointed at the sky.

Yoninah snuck a sideways glance at the sun. It was no longer a bright circle. A third of the sun was obscured by a dark shadow.

"My gods!" said Yoninah. "I have heard of such things. My, the birds, they are so quiet."

The other animals were quiet too. Goats, sheep, donkeys in their quarters in the neighboring houses, they all fell silent. There was a lull over the land. The unnatural darkness of what should have been a bright morning, and the silence of the animals led to an eerie quiet. Everyone was holding their breath, waiting to find out if the world was coming to an end.

"Is the sun going to come back?" asked the girls.

"It should come back," said their mother. Although she had personally never witnessed such an event before, she was certainly hoping it would come back.

The day grew even darker. By what should have been late morning, the sun was completely obscured by whatever shadow was attacking it. It felt like evening. The birds and other animals remained silent.

Finally, the sun started coming back. The unnatural darkness began to dissipate.

After another interval, the day had fully returned. It was a normal spring morning again. Except by now, it was noon. The donkeys were back to braying and the birds were back to flying. However, Yoninah couldn't shake an unsteady feeling.

"If the sun could disappear, what other ill-omens are in store for the city?" Yoninah thought to herself.

****

At the Palace

From the terrace of his palace apartment, Thut-Moses watched the birds flying overhead. A well-educated scribe from the court of the Egyptian pharaoh, he knew this was an annual, springtime ritual: flocks of birds migrating from Africa to their breeding grounds north of the Great Sea.

Thut-Moses was a tall man, with the ebony skin of his native land of Nubia. He was the king's eunuch, scribe, and aide. He and the king were the same age, in their mid- thirties. .

He had been in the King's service for the last fifteen years. When King Ammurabi had requested a scribe to be sent form the Egyptian court, a twenty-year-old Thut-Moses had sailed to Ugarit. In the intervening years, the eunuch had gained the King's trust. He came to enjoy his friendship with the King. He also enjoyed the privileges of life in the palace: good meals, fine robes to wear, and a personal attendant.

Thut-Moses continued to watch the spectacle in the sky. Then something unexpected happened. The day began to grow dark. Even though the sky was cloudless, the light of the sun was disappearing.

With a stab of fear running through him—celestial omens were to be taken seriously; he knew this from his years in Pharaoh's court-- Thut-Moses sent his attendant to the King's quarters. To tell him of this unholy darkening of the daytime sky. To come quickly to the courtyard, to see for himself.

A short while later, In the Grand Courtyard, the scribe met the King. With him was his bodyguard and the court astrologer.

Thut-Moses greeted the King and his entourage. King Ammurabi, as usual, made a striking appearance. He was almost as tall as his scribe. He had the full black beard and full head of hair of the royal lineage. He had the finely etched facial features of his father and grandfather. He wore the splendid robes reserved for royalty: with the purple stripe running along its length. The astrologer, meanwhile, was a short man wearing the traditional tunic of the Egyptians.

The King asked Thut-Moses, "What is this celestial event that requires my attention?"

The astrologer held a piece of tinted glass in his hand. Using the glass as a filter, he looked at the sun. After a few moments, he said: "The sun is indeed being attacked! This is what I was afraid of. There is a crescent of darkness on one side. That is why the day is growing dark. We have ancient scrolls in Egypt warning us of this event. We interpret it to mean that the serpent of chaos is attacking Ra, the god of the sun."

He gave the glass to the King. "It is safe to look at the sun if you use this glass. You will see for yourself: a black shadow is overtaking the sun."

Taking the glass and looking skyward, the King exclaimed. "Oh my gods, you are right!"

Thut-Moses looked as well. And nodded his agreement: the sight was unearthly.

It got darker and darker. The blanket of birds stopped flying. They settled on nearby rooftops and trees. It felt like dusk by now. The birds were apparently settling down for the night.

The Egyptian pontificated. "If we are fortunate, the attack will be short-lived, and the sun will return."

"What if we are unfortunate?" Thut-Moses asked.

"Then the world ends, my lord," the astrologer said.

With an existential threat added to the situation, they could do nothing except wait to see if the world ended. When the sun was entirely obscured by the dark shadow, the astrologer started reciting prayers to the gods. The prayers were in Egyptian, which Thut-Moses could understand. Thut-Moses recognized it as a powerful incantation. The darkness persisted and deepened such that one could pick out the stars in what seemed to be the nighttime sky. There was just darkness and the astrologer's recitation. Then a sliver of sun reappeared. Finally, after some anxious moments, the full sun emerged from the black stain covering it. And the day was normal again. The birds even started flying again.

The King and Thut-Moses both expressed relief that the sun had fully returned.

The Egyptian felt compelled to offer a further warning, however. "An attack on the sun is an omen of a coming war, my liege." The Egyptian's voice dropped to a lower octave as if underscoring the importance of his pronouncement.

Taking this information in hand, the King thanked the Egyptian for his help and waved him away.

The King took Thut-Moses' arm as they retreated to the shaded halls of the Palace. "Our city is surrounded by strong walls. We are at peace with our neighbors. I am not overly concerned," he said.

Thut-Moses noted that the King appeared untroubled by celestial omens. Still, he thought: "An omen is not to be ignored. And the sun disappearing was surely a bad sign.".

CHAPTER 2: PALACE STREET

In the Lower City

Two days later, Yoninah and her daughter Bat-El were walking hand in hand along Palace Street. It was a fine day in early spring. The winter rains were behind them. The trees were just beginning to send out tentative buds.

This was their favorite day of the week. They would make this trip weekly. As a healer in the lower city, Yoninah had to buy fresh medicinal plants for her shop.

Yoninah used to make this shopping trip with Laylah, her older daughter. Now that Laylah was all of fifteen, she left her behind, in charge of the healer's shop.

The two of them, mother and child, made a striking picture. Yoninah always dressed up for her shopping trips into the heart of the city. At age thirty-four, her hair was a lustrous black, curls caught up in a bronze hair ornament. She wore a tunic of fine Egyptian linen. She of course wore a veil on her face. All free women remained veiled. Only slaves and prostitutes went around with their faces unveiled.

Her daughter Bat-El at age ten was still too young to require a face covering on the street. Bat-El's bright eyes shone with anticipation at the trip down Palace Street.

Palace Street led from the bridge over the river Ed Delbeh, along which the sailors and merchants come from the Harbor. Running through the lower city, with its modest two-story houses and shops, the street climbed towards the Temple Mount, where the Palace and Temples stood.

As they made their way along Palace Street, Bat-El called out: "Oh look! There's the monkey man!" Tucked into a door stood a man with a monkey perched on his shoulder. The little monkey's hand was extended, to beg for coins or for treats. No bigger than a small sack of grain, it had black and white markings on its furry face and wore a little red hat with colorful ribbons.

"Can I give it a treat?" asked Bat El. Yoninah carried a bag of dates with her for just such an occasion. She gave her daughter two dates for the little primate. The monkey took the dates nimbly, chattering away as it expressed its gratitude.

"It must have come with the traders from Egypt," said Yoninah. "That's where monkeys come from."

While reluctant to leave the monkey behind, Bat-El noticed a group of sailors passing them. The young men were speaking a medley of languages -- mostly Ugarit, with its melodious sounds, a smattering of Egyptian, and an occasional phrase in Akkadian. The sailors' voices carried well across the length of the street.

There was also a rude Hittite bellowing at the shopkeepers. "Get me my donkey right away!" the Hittite said in guttural tones.

Finally, the mother and daughter heard entirely foreign sounds, those of Mycenae, from the islands of the Aegean and from Crete.

Palace Street was narrow, like all the streets in Ugarit, with stone and mud brick houses bounding it on either side. Contained within its narrow margins was a wealth of color and sound.

Bat-El found herself beguiled. Wearing multicolored long skirts with bells on them, a slave girl ran past. Priestesses, modestly veiled, made their way back to the Temple Quarter.

Dogs barked in the garbage. All these sounds added to the acoustic chaos of the street.

Passing shops at the lower end of the street, mother and child lingered at their favorite vendors. Bat-El and Yoninah especially enjoyed the shop that sold execration pots, which were red pots inscribed with lively curses written in black script. Customers would hold one of these execration pots so inscribed, recite the curse out loud so the gods could hear, and then smash it to activate the curse.

"Who do you want to curse today?" the shopkeeper called out to passerby. "We have a nice selection of 'Curse the Egyptians' or 'Should the foreigners flounder and sink!'"

Lingering at a shop that sold terracotta figures of household gods, Yoninah admired the curvaceous figure of Asherah. The goddess of fertility, the protectress of women and children, she was by far the most popular of the household gods. And Yoninah's personal favorite.

Yoninah and Bat-El's progress up Palace Street halted when they came to a cluster of people in the road. They were gathered around a wildly gesticulating figure, a man with long gray hair and a disheveled appearance.

"Hear, hear! Lord Baal told me the city is doomed!" the man called to the crowd.

The man's gray hair was wild, his beard long and untrimmed. He wore a tunic which looked none the better for wear. His torso was wiry with the gaunt appearance of someone who did not eat enough. Yoninah thought he probably fasted. A mechanism by which many of these self-proclaimed prophets achieved their visions.

"The city is doomed!" The prophet lifted his arms to the sky when he spoke of Baal. "Lord Baal spoke to me. I was asleep and He sent me a vision. I heard a great and mighty wind blowing. Then I felt an earthquake come and shake everything. Then I saw a fire burning-- the fire covered the land and burnt it to the ground! Then Lord Baal spoke to me! His voice was like no other's: booming and deep."

Yoninah looked around at the crowd. Many of the onlookers appeared skeptical...

"Thus spoke Lord Baal," the prophet proclaimed. 'Tell the people of Ugarit: they have failed to honor my House. They have failed to make burnt offerings in My Temple, nor have they made sacrifices. They have done evil. Tell them: You will hear the rams' horns blowing—the blasts of war. The walls of the city will topple. From the sound of archers and from raised swords, you will flee. You will raise up a lament, a dirge among the women. The city will be destroyed. The enemy will come and attack the land of Ugarit, delivering those destined to captivity, to captivity. And those destined for the sword, to the sword.' "

Yoninah and Bat-El were impressed with his grand hand gestures and the vividness of his vision. Others on the street laughed at him.

"You have lost your mind, old man!" one man shouted.

"No, my eyes are clear, my mind is working perfectly. This was the vision of that our Lord Baal sent to me," the prophet replied.

The people, some muttering, "He is mad," went on their way. No one paid him much mind. The sun in a clear sky, the colors of spring flowers bright around them, the women in their flowing tunics, the young sailors with their boasts and jeers.

Yoninah thought the prophet was a gifted storyteller with a touch of madness, no doubt. She briefly remembered the birds settling out of the sky and the unnatural darkness the other. day. The memory gave her a brief sense of unease. She and Bat-El nonetheless continued their trip along Palace Street. It was hard to give much credence to a prophecy of doom, not when the city was prosperous, and their gates were well-guarded.

As they climbed the gentle incline of Palace Street, they approached the more prosperous houses near Temple Mount. The sounds of birds in the palm trees that lined the road, in these more refined neighborhoods, added to the auditory overload.

The houses were more spacious, the road a bit wider, with a finer class of customers. The shops at this end sold fine jewelry of gold and copper. Some bracelets had gemstones of jade, ruby, or turquoise from far away.

The Temple and its shops were located at the very highest point of the city. As they looked down, they could see the harbor below, with the waves of the Great Sea glistening in the sun. They could see three ships in the waters: their sails unfurled, catching the sea winds and heading away from the city.

On a quiet back street near the Temple, Yoninah and Bat-El found the vendor they sought. Sailors brought him wares they had smuggled into the city. Although trade was supposed to go directly to the Palace, to the King's accountants, there was always a trade in medicinal plants that came through the back door.

Carefully handing over the half-shekels in her purse and watching while the merchant weighed the silver pieces on his scales, Yoninah bought her requisite medicinal herbs: poppy seeds, cannabis flowers, valerian root, and mandrake root.

As Yoninah picked out the stock, she told her younger daughter what each herb treated. "Poppy seed for pain, cannabis for feeling nervous and jumpy, valerian root for sleep." She did not tell her daughter about the uses for mandrake root. She did not want to explain an aphrodisiac to the child.

With their purchases in hand, mother and child made their way back down Palace Street. The day had been lovely, a respite from the winter rains and the summer heat which was yet to come. Nothing like a spring day in the city. Altogether a successful trip, Yoninah thought with satisfaction. Although she could have done without the mad prophet.

CHAPTER 3: THE KING'S FEAST

A week after the unnatural darkening of the sun –the serpent god's attack on the god of the sun, according to the Egyptian astrologer—Thut-Moses and the King had mostly put the event behind them. More pressing matters demanded their attention. To wit, a royal feast.

The kingdom was hosting a grand feast in the Great Hall of the Palace. Prominent diplomats and merchants from neighboring kingdoms were invited. Most had arrived by ship. Spring began the season for commerce and travel on the Great Sea. The spring winds were kinder to sailing vessels than the storms of winter.

Thut-Moses, as the King's scribe and aide, would be the King's eyes and ears for the event and would make sure that everything went smoothly. The King trusted him. He knew that he had won the King's trust by always being deferential in speech, always careful of the King's feelings. The Nubian had been taught well at the scribal school, which had educated him in the ways of courtly life as well as in languages.

As the various diplomats and their aides gathered in the Great Hall, Thut-Moses welcomed them at the door. He made a memorable sight, with his height, ebony skin, and his fine robe of many colors. His features were even and pleasing. His face was clean-shaven. In fact, as a eunuch, his face was always clean-shaven. Eunuchs were unable to grow facial hair.

****

At the dinner party, Thut-Moses brought the visitors to where the King sat, on a fine chair at one end of the hall. As the King stood to greet his visitors, Thut-Moses noted that His Majesty made a fine picture, dressed his royal robes with their stripes of purple. Although Thut-Moses did notice a few ceases adorning the King's otherwise pristine forehead.

"It is a pleasure to see so many friends sitting down together for a feast! We are pleased to welcome Uriah, the noble emissary from Carchemesh and the Hittite court; Kittim, the honorable envoy of the king of Cyprus; and Potifar, trade envoy from the court of the Pharoah in Egypt," the King said.

Behind the King, Thut-Moses could see the colorful fresco on the wall. Done in the Minoan style, the fresco showed leaping dolphins, an octopus, and exotic fishes. The fresco, at least one hundred years old, was painted during the reign of King Ammurabi's grandfather.

Sadly, the Minoans were gone. Thut-Moses knew there were no more artists who could paint with that level of skill. Moving into their palaces and taking over their trade routes, the Myceneans had displaced the Minoans. Perhaps a lesson to be learned about the transient nature of empires and powerful kingdoms in the Mediterranean, Thut-Moses thought to himself. But that was one observation he would never share with King Ammurabi.

As the usual babble of voices started up, with the conversations between one diplomat and another, Thut-Moses took a moment to appreciate the luxury of the event. The palace had enough treasures on display to impress foreign dignitaries with Ugarit's level of sophistication: golden statuettes of Baal, a bronze head of a bull with horns of gold, intricately designed pottery from the Aegean. There were potted palm trees and chattering monkeys scampering in their branches.

Thut-Moses was pleased to note how impressed the guests were by their surroundings. He felt a tinge of anxiety, however. The envoy from Cyprus was navigating a quarrel about a ship taken hostage in Egyptian-held territory in Canaan. Thut-Moses hoped a spirit of brotherhood would envelop the group. There were armed guards at the doors, just in case.

As dusk was falling, torches were lit in the hall. Each guest was comfortably seated on a bench or low chair. Goatskins softened the seats. Small tables appeared, upon which serving girls brought out plates of cheeses, olives, and bread. The cup boy poured wine into gold goblets. Then another server came, with plates of kid goat meat prepared in goat milk. The cup boy kept the wine cups full.

A bard and acrobats performed for the guests as they dined. The bard strumming his lyre, the acrobats tumbling and dancing.

As a final touch, serving girls brought out pomegranates, figs, and dates for dessert. The guests looked quite sated. The last course was wine that would finish off the evening as the guests enjoyed the entertainment.

****

David the Bard

Strumming on his lyre, David, the King's bard had provided quiet background music for the diners. Now he took center-stage—in the center of the ring of chairs and tables-- and prepared to sing and play his instrument as the after-dinner entertainment. With dark curly hair, flashing dark eyes, and a charming smile, David was a handsome young man. Thut-Moses smiled as he looked at David, as the bard's antics often amused him.

Thut-Moses knew that the King's favorite part of any dinner party was the entertainment that followed. He would drink a goblet of sweet red wine and listen to David play his lyre and sing songs of praise to the gods or other lively melodies.

Also enjoying the music were the two royal wives---arrayed in their finery and jewels, Thut-Moses thought the two of them looked splendid.

The younger wife was dressed in a blue robe from the seamstresses of Egypt. With her black hair swept up in an ornate bronze pin, with her eyes done in the Egyptian style-- heavily outlined in kohl—she made a fine addition to the evening.

The First Wife looked even more resplendent. She was dressed to the height of fashion, with her auburn hair carefully styled into elaborate curls, wearing a fine linen tunic with a generous display of cleavage; her arms adorned with gold bracelets; and her neck glistening with a necklace made with gemstones of amber, jade, and emeralds.

Thut-Moses liked this Queen. He admired not only her beauty, but also her intelligence. They had lively conversations about palace politics. A daughter of the King of Amurru, a neighboring kingdom, she had grown up in another palace, enmeshed in rumors of Hittite aggressions on their borders; of piracy threatening their seaports. She was knowledgeable about the hazards of ruling a kingdom.

The King and Queen had been together ever since her father had arranged the match. They had produced four children. Three of them—two boys and a girl-- had so far survived the usual hazards of childhood, The King also had two children from his second wife. The King had plenty of children. Thut-Moses was grateful. He was well-aware of the value of viable heirs when it came to maintaining the stability of a kingdom.

After a brief prayer to Baal , there followed a bawdy love song from the Egyptians. Thut-Moses appreciated the subtlety of this arrangement. An Egyptian love song made an excellent bridge between the different countries represented by his guests. It provided a means of crossing all cultural boundaries and appealing to Hittite, Cypriote, and Egyptian alike. The ballad named body parts and expressed endless yearning on the part of the young lovers.

Seated in front of the group, David strummed s a few notes on the lyre. A young woman appeared. With brown skin, slender arms and legs, and a fine-boned face, she appeared Ethiopian. Dressed in a tunic of the finest linen, nearly translucent, in the Egyptian style; she wore a red scarf around her hips, with small bells attached. The dancer proved a mesmerizing sight as she undulated the music.

She started singing, with David playing the lyre. Her voice was clear and strong. She danced to the music as well, with movements of her hands, swaying of her hips, and tapping of her bare feet.

> *I am dark, from the desert, baked dark in the desert sun.*
>
> *But my beloved, he seeks me out, he calls me.*
>
> *Where is my beloved? I go to look for him.*
>
> *He is tall like the cedars of Lebanon. His legs are like pillars of fine marble.*

His hair is black with wondrous curls. His lips are ripe like a pomegranate.

I seek him in the streets. I seek him in the gardens.

Have you seen him, O daughters of the city?

My heart yearns for his touch. My ears ache for the sound of his voice.

Then David strummed another chord from the lyre and started to sing the man's part. The young woman continued to dance and to look at him with adoration. Whether real or feigned, it was convincing.

My beloved, you are fair. My own, my bride

Your lips are red like rubies, their taste as sweet as wine.

Your breasts are like two fawns, twins of a gazelle.

Let us go for a walk among the lilies, when the wind blows gently,

And the shadows flee.

Let us go to the mount of myrrh, to the hill of frankincense.

Arise, my darling My fair one, come away!

The guests asked for an encore. The duo obliged, with the young woman's voice alternating with David's. She would sing a verse and then he would reply with a verse.

Thut-Moses silently said a prayer that David and the lissome young woman were not involved in any extra-marital liaison. He feared for the safety of his friend. David's new wife was a force to be reckoned with. She would not take kindly to an affair.

Sometimes Thut-Moses was grateful he was a eunuch. Not that he had any choice in the matter.

The evening wound down after that. Pleasantries were being exchanged all around. The diplomats were heading off to the chambers provided for them, for the duration of their stay in the kingdom.

The emissary from Cyprus had been drinking red wine steadily throughout the evening. He had been talking about his adventures as a young man about town, which were now years in the past. When he stood up to go, the Cypriot's face was flushed and his gait unsteady. He put his hand on the shoulder of a serving girl with long black hair and flashing teeth, smooth arms and legs on ample display under her shift.

"Sweets, meet me later?" The girl wriggled away from his grasping hand. Thut-Moses had a manservant, conveniently armed, walk the inebriate to his room "to make sure he gets there safely." The young serving girl flashed Thut-Moses a relieved smile.

The King was evidently pleased with the evening, Thut-Moses watched as he bid his wives good night and went off to spend time with a young concubine, which was a predictable effect of the Egyptian love poems.

CHAPTER 4: AT THE HEALER'S SHOP

Yoninah's house had the classic sign of the healer outside the door: a snake entwined around a pole.

In the courtyard of the house, Yoninah and her older daughter, Laylah, drew heavy buckets of water from the well. They always did the wash on First Day. The late morning sun warmed up the stone pavement of the courtyard.

Laylah, at age fifteen, was a startlingly pretty girl. She had even started wearing kohl on her eyes and rouge on her cheeks.

Adding clothes to the water, Yoninah and Laylah started the serious work of scrubbing with sand to get the dirt off, then stomping with their feet for further traction, and finally rinsing.

As they emptied the wash water in the drain under the stairs, Laylah started talking about all the handsome sailors she had seen on Palace Street in the last few days. The ships were starting to come back into the harbor, after a winter lull. Yoninah thought Laylah would need to find a husband soon. After all, Yoninah married at age seventeen.

Joining them in the courtyard, the ten-year-old started teasing her older sister.

"You think all the boys are handsome," Bat-El said.

"No, I don't," Laylah said. "I think Nefesh-El is ugly."

"Well, that is true," said the little one. Their neighbor, Nefesh-El was an unfortunate specimen of manhood: too skinny, all bone and sinew, no muscle.

Hearing a firm knock at the door from the street, Yoninah wiped her wet hands on her skirt and answered the door. A middle-aged man stood there, nursing his left arm. The arm was clearly crooked.

"I broke my arm. Can you fix it?" he said with a slight accent.

"I am the healer. Yes, I can splint your arm for you," she said. "And I have pain meds for you as well."

"That would be most welcome." He grimaced with the pain.

Showing him to the front room, where she kept her herbs and supplies, she got him situated on a comfortable bench. She was skilled at setting broken bones. Every month or so, someone from the docks appeared at her door with an injury to an arm or leg. The men did heavy work: unloading cargo from the ships, carrying it to the storehouse, and laying it carefully. Clay jars full of grain were heavy, and even heavier when filled with wine. The dockworkers also lifted tin ingots from Afghanistan and copper ingots from Cyprus. All too often, something fell and caught a stray arm or leg on the way.

"I have silver to pay you. I am told you are good at your work. I've broken bones before. I know it will lay me up for a while." The man attempted a smile, but it didn't quite work.

Looking more closely at him, she saw that he had the cheekbones, chin, and beard of the Aegean. His hair was black, mixed with a sprinkling of gray. The skin of his face and arms was heavily tanned, with creases across the face, courtesy of the harsh sun of the Great Sea. A handsome face except for the grimace.

Probably a refugee from the war in the north, from Troy, she thought. A war that had been over and done with for a good twenty years. She washed the wounded arm and went to her shelves for further supplies. On the way, she passed a shrine to the Goddess Asherah. The goddess – as cast in bronze with details rendered in gold highlights-- sat on a pedestal, near her shelves. A ceremonial bronze bowl sat nearby.

Pouring wine into the bronze bowl, she quietly made libations to the goddess. She silently offered a prayer: "Oh, Queen of Heaven, who gives skill to the healer and comfort to those who are in pain, take this libation of wine."

She picked up a salve of poppy seed extract and myrrh and returned to the bench where the Mycenean sat. She gently washed and applied a compress with the numbing ointment to his arm. As she worked, she made small talk to distract him from his pain,

"I'm guessing you are Mycenaean. Not much accent there, but you look like you're from the Aegean. I am guessing you work on the docks. How did you break your arm?"

"I was carrying wine jars on a cart drawn by an ox. Everything was going well when the creature took a tumble," said the Mycenean. "The cursed animal found the only hole in the path and lost his footing. I tried to catch the jars before they hit the ground. The jars survived but my arm broke. Heard the thing snap. Hurts like the sting of a thousand bees."

"Well, let the compress work for a bit. The compress should numb it up in just a few more minutes. Let me find a splint to fit you."

"And maybe a cup of honeyed wine to take the edge off?" he asked,

"Certainly," she said. Yoninah called for her daughter Laylah to fetch a cup of wine with honey added.

Yoninah found, among her supplies, a length of wood planking and some clean linen dressings and laid these on the table where the Mycenean sat. She sat down as well and engaged him in conversation. An important skill, while waiting for the numbing medicine to take hold.

"How did you end up in Ugarit? This is a distance from the Aegean Sea," Yoninah asked.

"The war," he said flatly. "I mean the Trojan War. I joined the navy in Mycenae when I was seventeen because I thought it would be a grand adventure. They paid a good bonus as well. "

"Ten stinking years later – most of it spent outside the grand walls of Troy, in a siege that was going nowhere – we somehow broke through the walls and razed and looted and burnt the city."

"I was sick of the whole adventure by then. And sick of the sea: too many storms, too many shipwrecks. Never wanted to go back across the Great Sea."

"Is my arm almost ready? I can't feel the pain anymore."

"Good," she said. "Lay your arm flat on the table. And here is that wine for you.".

Taking the cup of wine from Laylah with his right arm, he drank it down in one fell swoop. He was clearly not an epicurean.

Yoninah asked her daughter to stay. She wanted to show her how to set a broken bone. She described to her each step, as she proceeded with setting it aright.

As he laid his misshapen left arm down on the table, Yoninah took hold of the forearm just below the elbow. She wrapped her other hand around his wrist and gave a forceful pull-- the goal being to nudge the wayward bones back into position.

Hearing a click as the edges went together, Yoninah was pleased. She said to Laylah: "You can hear and feel the click when the bone goes back into position." The arm was straight again. She had Laylah apply the splint and wrap it in cloth and tie it firmly in position.

"Not bad. Maybe some more of that wine would help." He looked a bit pale, so Yoninah poured him a second cup, a bit smaller than the first.

"It feels pretty good, considering." The man's attempt at a smile proved a bit more successful

"You fought at Troy. That's a goodly distance from Ugarit," Yoninah said as she gathered up a sling. "How did you wind up here?"

"Never wanted to go back to the open sea. Took passage on a ship bound for Ugarit. As you know, those ships travel along the coast. No more open water for me! That took a scant ten days, what with favorable winds and currents. Been here a good twenty years now," he said.

"Here are some extra salve and cloths.," she said. "The ointment should help with pain. Wrap the arm with the plank in position. You'll need to change the dressing every couple of days."

Showing him a length of cloth folded into a triangular shape, she continued her instructions. "Here's an arm sling. Let me wrap it around your arm. It needs to be tied at the neck, to keep the elbow bent and close against your chest."

As she tied the sling around his neck, he stared at her chest.

"That's a pretty necklace you are wearing." His eyes were fixed on the pendant she wore, a painted terracotta figure of a naked woman.

Yoninah bit her lip as she tried to hold back a smile. Her patient was a bit tipsy now.

"Thank you. It is Asherah, the Queen of Heaven." She was momentarily distracted by the intensity of his gaze. She reverted quickly to her healer persona.

"There you go. No using the arm! For at least four weeks, probably six weeks. It takes that long for breaks to heal. If you try to use it too soon, it will easily fracture again. Will you be able to rest the arm for a month?"

"Guess I'll have to be," he said.

"Do you have a wife or daughter to keep an eye on you? Help with the arm, cook your meals?" Yoninah couldn't meet his eyes as she asked this question.

"No," he said. "My wife died. My son lives a few days from here. But I have a friend who can help. I'll be all right."

"My husband died five years ago," Yoninah said before she could catch herself. She didn't really need to tell him this information. She turned away and busied herself for a moment.

"I need you to come back in two weeks," she said. "I'll need to make sure the arm is healing."

"My name is Menelaus. And yours is?"

"You can call me Yoninah," she said.

Giving her a silver shekel for the arm repair, he swore he would be careful with the arm and agreed to return in two weeks. He gave her a lopsided grin at that point. Possibly due to the excess of wine, she thought.

After he left, she felt uplifted. That had been an unusually pleasant interaction. The bone had gone smoothly back into place.

Laylah had remained respectful while the Mycenean was there. After he left, she looked at her mother's flushed face and laughed. "You like him." she said. Yoninah agreed: "He is handsome enough. He kept us amused." She thought, "It is true, I am looking to forward to seeing him again."

****

In the next week or two, there were the usual customers. There was the young wife seeking an aphrodisiac for her middle-aged husband; the courtesan seeking an abortion after a liaison; and the angry merchant seeking a curse on the entire nation of Egypt.

She gave them what she had, in her closet of wonders: dried mandrake root for the flagging husband; an ergot pessary for the courtesan; and an execration stone for the angry merchant who hated the Egyptians.

Yoninah would hear her mother's voice as she treated her clients. Her mother died the year before. She had taught her daughter everything she knew about the healing arts.

As Yoninah sees a young sailor with a dislocated shoulder, she would hear her mother say: "Oooh! He is handsome! Pull his arm just so and the shoulder will be back in position. He'll be back in the brothels in no time."

Or, for the young woman who was newly pregnant and complaining of frequent nausea: "Ah, the vomiting! The special tea should do the trick. But no more than a spoonful, if you give too much, she will get glassy-eyed and sleepy."

Or for the man who was complaining of enemies seeking him out and plotting against him day and night, she would say: "He is losing his mind. He is seeing and hearing things that are not there. Send him to the priests and priestesses. They can give drugs to cause visions. Sometimes these medicines help with whatever madness has seized him."

Her mother always had strong opinions on the right and wrong ways to treat the complaints of those with physical or mental pain. Her opinions were usually helpful.

An altogether usual week or two in the shop. Little did she know things were changing.

CHAPTER 5: THUT-MOSES—THE EUNUCH'S JOURNEY

The King and David sometimes teased Thut-Moses for his status as a eunuch. Did he not feel that he was missing out on something? Thut-Moses dealt with these gibes good-naturedly.

Thut Moses did not mind being a eunuch. He knew that eunuchs were highly prized as courtiers. Besides their obvious inability to impregnate women in the harem, they made excellent advisors and guards and aides to the court. Their emotions were less volatile than those of full-fledged men, their judgment unfettered by lust or by the heat of jealousy.

He had been taken captive at age ten, in one of the many conflicts between Nubia and Egypt. As a child, he was brought to the court in Thebes. A handsome boy, he was first intended as an attendant in the royal harem. The women of the harem preferred pretty boys as attendants, so Thut-Moses was castrated.

Fortunately, the surgeon performing the castration was skilled. He drugged the child generously beforehand and during the weeks it took to recover. Thut-Moses did not remember the surgery at all.

When it was later discovered that he was a bright child and a quick study, his career path took a sharp turn. Instead of going to the harem, Thut-Moses was sent to the school for scribes.

Thut-Moses would sometimes think about his early years in the scribal school in Egypt. He knew that he had been singled out, that being chosen as a scribal student was a great honor. He took to his studies with enthusiasm. He was adept at languages. He learned how to write in Egyptian hieratics. The script, written on papyrus, consisted of 600 characters, and was used for all official documents. Learning to read and write opened a whole new world to him.

He copied the works of the physicians from a thousand years before. He copied the Book of the Dead and the stories about gods and goddesses. He would lose himself in these stories.

He also studied the Akkadian script, used for trade throughout the Great Sea. Finally he picked up Ugaritic: a cleverly devised, entirely phonetic script of 30 letters. This was a trivial endeavor, compared to learning how to scribe in Egyptian and Akkadian.

When he was twenty years old, the king of Ugarit sent a missive to the Pharoah, asking if he had a skilled scribe he could send to Ugarit. Thut-Moses traveled to the court of a young Ammurabi. He remembered the voyage from Egypt to Ugarit. His heart had soared with the open sky over the sea. They had taken a boat made in Byblos for the voyage. The boats made in Byblos were the best in the known world, more sea-worthy than the boats made in Egypt. Thut-Moses enjoyed the dolphins leaping in the water alongside the ship. He also enjoyed the novelty of being surrounded by sailors and traders from the land of the Canaanites.

He remembered being excited by all of it. He was young enough, in hindsight, that he had no fear of the sea. He had no concept of death and drowning. Fears would come later when he was older. Back then, it was all a grand adventure.

When he first met the King, Thut-Moses was comforted by all the Egyptian touches in the Palace: the columns of cedar of Lebanon, painted with irises and seabirds from the Nile, the

Egyptian style pool in the courtyard with its potted papyrus plants. He could see the relationship between their goddess they called Astarte and the Egyptian goddess Isis. He especially enjoyed hearing the love poems from Egypt even if his own gender was undefined.

He would listen when Egyptian envoys came before the King. He could translate for them. The King quickly promoted him to his aide, in addition to being his scribe.

Thut-Moses enjoyed the high status he held in the court and his comfortable quarters in the palace. He knew he could even marry, if he chose. Although he could have children only through adoption.

He grew to read the King's expressions and to respect him. Not just fear him as the ultimate arbiter of justice in the court. He grew to like the man and his First Wife.

He thought, "I am content as a scribe and aide to this King."

****

Thut-Moses and his friend David would sometimes meet for conversation and drinks at the tavern in the lower city. They would dress in simple clothes and leave behind the ornate gold chains they otherwise wore. Although Thut-Moses had the dark skin of the Nubian and would tower over the other men at the bar, they could pretend they were incognito.

At these get-togethers. David would share with Thut-Moses his escapades with various women. Thut-Moses would listen, and think David was too attractive for his own good. He had told David as much at times. Women kept throwing themselves at him, which Thut-Moses feared would lead to serious problems.

Some six months prior, they had been on one of their forays to the lower city tavern, David had shared with Thut-Moses that he was involved in a rather touchy situation. He was seeing the General's wife. While the General was away. Thut-Moses had advised David to break off their secret liaison. But David was in love. Or in lust; so hard to tell the difference. She was a beautiful woman, with a curvaceous, soft body and healthy appetites.

And then all sorts of chaos arose. When the General made an unexpected return to Ugarit. As David related the story to Thut-Moses, he said, "Jezebel and I were certainly not expecting him." They were enmeshed with their passions in her bedchamber when the guard at her door announced the General's return.

David made a hasty retreat. He escaped to the terrace, just outside the bed chamber. Clinging naked to the edge of the terrace, he dangled precariously twelve feet from the ground. This was on the second floor. He looked for a way to climb down. The General barged into the bedchamber. David could hear his thundering voice.

Desperate to evade the general's notice, David opted to simply drop the distance. He fell clumsily and broke an ankle. Unfortunately, the general heard his scream outside the window. The guards rushed to find David outside the window. The guards bound his ankle, then they threw clothes on him and tossed him in jail.

At this point in David's retelling of the story, Thut-Moses burst into laughter. Even now, some months later, he could not help but smile when he recalled the image of David dangling from the edge of the terrace without benefit of clothing.

The King had gotten involved, arranging David's release from prison and insisting the General divorce his wife without killing her or David. Compensating the General for his pain, the King gave him a large bribe. Finally, the King ordered David to marry his paramour. The matter was finally resolved, and David was free to return as musician for the King. Although the bard limped for a while.

****

On this trip to their favorite tavern—a good six months after the Affair of the Broken Ankle—David had some news to share. Drinking down a beer, he announced: "My wife is pregnant. She is excited, but I'm not so excited. I have no ambitions of being a father."

"Perhaps you do not know where babies come from?" Thut-Moses couldn't help teasing his friend. "This cannot be a complete surprise, after all."

"She has gotten more seductive lately! I can hardly keep up with her. She expects to have relations every night. I am getting tired, to tell you the truth.".

Thut-Moses smiled at him. He found it difficult to feel sorry for the man. They sipped their beers in amiable silence for a few minutes.

David told him he had to send back home the pretty girl with whom he sang the Egyptian love songs. His wife had caught them in an amorous embrace and had insisted that the girl be sent away. David was under strict orders not to hire anyone who was young and pretty for the performance. Which led him into a dilemma: who would want to listen to or look at someone who was old and ugly?

The tavern was getting crowded by this point. The lamps were being lit. Thut-Moses and David listened in on the conversations around them.

Their talk was typical for a group of men. The younger men were quite drunk. They had just come into the harbor. After being at sea for a few weeks, they were happy to drink beer and eat hot soup on solid ground for a change. The older men were mostly sober. Usually dockworkers with families in Ugarit, the older men were having a beer or two before heading home.

Thut-Moses noticed a middle-aged man, with the heft and height of a soldier from Mycenae. He thought, "I bet he can lift cargo like the youngsters." Then he noticed a splint on the man's arm. The Mycenean came to his table and said, "It's a pleasure meeting you and the bard. Your fame precedes you…" The tumult in the tavern was such that others did not hear the man's words. But Thut-Moses did and understood that his disguise did not work fully. He put his hand on the man's good arm and said, "The pleasure is mine! Your name is?"

The man answered, "Menelaus," with a broad smile. And they nodded amicably to one another. The city was small enough, thought Thut-Moses, that secret identities do not stay secret for long. The older man returned to his table.

The men in the bar started singing an old song that sailors had sung for ages. They were terribly off-key. David could not resist jumping in, to try to get then up to a reasonable facsimile of the correct key. The sailors were duly impressed by his musical skills. They sang a whole medley of songs, with David as one of their numbers. They bought David and his friend beers.

They asked Thut-Moses where he hailed from.

"Egypt," Thut-Moses replied. The Nubians had close relations with the Egyptians. A Nubian from Egypt was a common sight. The sailors offered Thut-Moses a toast that he should get safely back home. They assumed he was a traveling envoy.

Thut-Moses nodded amicably at their good wishes. And thought to himself that he would like to return to Egypt at some point. Suddenly, he missed the reeds of the Delta, the birds of the Nile, and the luxuries of the Pharoah's grand palace.

David and Thut-Moses made their way back to the Palace, still a bit inebriated but not to such an extent that they were a danger to themselves or to others. They made their way up along Palace Street. The night air was bracing. They carried a torch with them because the streets were dark at night. The two of them returned to the Palace gate without incident. The guard at the gate, an unpleasant older man, at first acted like he did not recognize them but he always acted like that. He eventually allowed them to pass.

CHAPTER 6: MENELAUS RETURNS TO THE HEALER'S SHOP

Two weeks later, at the healer's shop: Yoninah heard heavy knocking on the door from the street.

When she opened the door, there stood Menelaus. His arm still wrapped in a sling, but no longer grimacing from the pain. The color had returned to his face. He said his friend had kept him fed and kept the arm dressed.

She had him sit down in her workroom and took a nearby bench herself. He laid his arm on the table. As she carefully unwrapped the dressing, Yoninah noted that the arm looked good. The swelling was going away.

"It is healing fine," she said. "Looks nice and straight."

She applied more ointment for pain and changed the dressing. Giving him clean cloths and a fresh sling, she advised him to keep protecting the arm.

"No lifting for at least two more weeks." Yoninah told him in an authoritative voice..

He smiled at her tone. Yoninah decided his smile was slightly warmer than the medical interlude warranted. "Did you want a cup of wine?" she asked. "I have some time on my hands." That wasn't strictly true, as she had plenty to do, but she wasn't expecting any more patients.

"I would very much like a cup of wine," Menelaus replied.

Yoninah poured two cups of wine. "How are things going at the harbor?" she asked.

"The harbor is busy," he replied. "Now that the winter rains and adverse currents are behind us, the ships have started sailing again. Two days ago, we had a ship with grain from Egypt and a second ship setting sail for the Aegean. Cyprus should be sending us a shipload of copper in the next few days. We will transfer it to a ship bound for Miletus, the seaport that the Hittites use. Those Hittites, they have an endless appetite for copper, to mix with Afghani tin, to make their bronze weapons."

"Any news of pirates or raiders?" asked Yoninah. "My husband, he was a captain on a merchant ship. He used to say that there were often pirates in the Aegean.".

"There are always rumors of pirates in the Aegean Sea. Stray Myceneans take up piracy for a season every year. Usually after the planting is done, that is my impression. But I have not heard anything outside the usual," said Menelaus.

She told him about her husband: "His ship went down five years ago on a trip along the Aegean coast."

"Sorry to hear that," he said.

Nodding in acknowledgement of his offer of condolences, she was quiet for a moment.

"Come to dinner," she said. "The girls and I would welcome the company. Why don't you come next week on the feast day? We'll have goat to eat that day!"

****

Wearing a fresh tunic and with his beard trimmed, Menelaus returned for dinner the following week. His left arm still in a sling, he carried a gift of pomegranates in his good right arm. Yoninah greeted him at the door and led him to a low table set out on the roof-terrace where warm evening breezes blew.

They sat cross-legged on mats. The meal itself was the much-anticipated goat, cooked in goat's milk, with fresh bread and pomegranates for dessert. There was red wine for those over a certain age and watered-down wine for Bat-El.

Laylah kept smiling as she looked at Menelaus and then looked at her mother. There had been no dinner guests at their table for some time. She wasn't sure she remembered there ever being a male guest before.

Both girls peppered Menelaus with questions about the harbor.

"Tell us about the sailors!" Laylah said.

"It's mostly folk from Ugarit and from Byblos and Tyre in the harbor. Byblos and Tyre, they are Canaanites and speak much the same language that we speak in Ugarit. They are the best boat-makers in the world and the best sailors, too! The Egyptians can't hardly build a ship to sail the Great Sea. They buy boats from Byblos."

"The men from Byblos and Tyre are heavy drinkers and often get rowdy and start fighting," he continued. "In the taverns, they are also big talkers, at least before they start beating up on each other. They can tell you where the merchants' ships are heading, where the pirates are lurking on the high seas and what ships have gone down. There have been a few shipwrecks lately, up north. The Aegean coast is a bit tricky, what with the winds and shoals."

"What about the Egyptians?" Laylah asked.

"We get a few Egyptians on the boats. They are the clean-shaven ones. Mostly passengers on the boats-- emissaries from their Pharaoh, bringing messages back and forth. They seldom exchange words with the men in the harbor."

"What about the tall dark sailors?" Bat-El asked.

"Those are Nubians, from Africa. They share a border with Egypt. They go to Egypt to get work on the ships. They tell stories of great kingdoms in Nubia, rich in gold and ivory. They wear those ivory charms on their necks. They say it keeps them safe while traveling on the seas. They are a superstitious lot. And they love to play drums. Nothing like a bunch of drunk Nubian sailors, maybe with a drummer or two, dancing in a circle."

The girls were duly impressed with his reports from the harbor. They went off to finish their chores while Menelaus and Yoninah sat at the table and drank a second cup of wine. The conversation turned to Menelaus working on the docks.

"Do you like working at the docks?" Yoninah asked.

"I like the give and take at the docks," Menelaus said. "The conversations with other dockworkers and sailors, the bantering of the other men."

Yoninah touched his arm. "I am so sorry about your losing your wife."

"It's all right," Menelaus said. "At first, I was numb with grief. I started drinking too much. The Egyptians call beer the 'gift of the gods.' It made me forget my sorrow. After six months, I was finally able to wake up in the morning and not have to take a beer first thing. I would still go to the taverns. I have always enjoyed talking to folk over a beer. The sailors always have good stories to share. That took away some of my loneliness."

"Who is your friend who bandaged your arm?" Yoninah asked.

"His name is Tahir. He is a young fellow. He also works at the harbor. I met him two years ago. Him and his dog. He is originally from Afghanistan. He left the caravans when he was fifteen or so and decided he liked working in Ugarit well enough. I like him. He has a good heart. I'll have you meet him. He is quite a talker. He keeps me company."

"What did your wife die of?" Yonina asked gently.

"'The Egyptian plague, that's what we called it. That was four years ago, when it swept through our compound. Our boy lives outside the city, he wasn't exposed to it, thank the gods. There are so many ways, it seems, that a portal can open into the Underworld. The plague is one way."

"You have a son? Does he now live here in the city?" asked Yoninah.

"No, he lives in a small town some days into the mountains," Menelaus said. "He was sixteen when his mother died. He's been living with his uncle since he was twelve. His mother's brother took him in, to train him in the art of growing grapes and of making wine.. They have excellent vineyards there. He is all grown now and married. He has a child already. So, I have a grandson. The merchants who bring wine from this little town also bring me messages, so I know how they are doing."

"I'd better get going. Right nice of you to have me for dinner. You're the prettiest dinner companion I've had in a long time," he said.

Yoninah blushed.

CHAPTER 7: THUT-MOSES AND QUEEN DONITAYA

The First Wife and Thut-Moses had agreed to meet for a literary excursion in the Queen's quarters. Queen Donitaya was curious about Egyptian medicine. She felt the palace physician was pompous. He was so certain of his own superiority and that of Egyptian physicians in general. She wanted to know what it was about Egyptian medicine that made its practitioners so exceptional.

Menelaus thought to himself: The Queen's mother had died recently. The physician had attended her, treating her with amulets and incantations. He thought that the Queen was angry with the physician for his failure to cure her mother.

In any event, they were going to start by reading an Egyptian medical papyrus. Thut-Moses was friends with the Egyptian physician and had borrowed the scroll from him. He had promised the physician that he would guard it with his life.

He had carefully carried it, wrapped in an embroidered bag, to the Queen' apartments.

The Queen's quarters were in the east wing of the palace, as were the other living quarters for the royals. Thut-Moses had more modest quarters on the opposite side of the palace. To get to the royal quarters, he had to cross the Great Courtyard, a spacious plaza paved with smooth stones. He passed a fountain on the way which emptied into a shallow pool. He passed the gardens with shrubs just setting out buds, spikes of grasses, and a few trees providing welcome shade. He passed the pavilion, a roofed structure supported by four stout columns that were painted red. When Thut-Moses finally arrived at the imposing doors that led into the east wing, he was met by a guard standing sentry.

The guard was formidable in appearance, both for the spear he carried and his stern demeanor. The guard sported a trimmed black beard flecked with gray. The rugged career of a soldier was etched into his features. Despite his gruff exterior, he recognized Thut-Moses and gave a brief smile. The guard lowered his spear and allowed Thut-Moses to enter.

Inside the door was a generous stone staircase leading to the upper story. All the living quarters were on the second floor. Thut-Moses climbed the stairs and knocked on the door to the

Queen's apartment. A female attendant ushered him into her front room, where she saw visitors.

This was the first time that Thut-Moses had been to the Queen's apartment. He saw that the walls of her drawing room were plastered over and painted with a bright yellow wash. A blue frieze ran the length of the room, done in the classic Minoan design of waves of the sea. There were fine chairs, adorned with sheepskin for comfort and matching footstools

As he entered, Thut-Moses also took note of the greenery in the room. In alcoves along the walls were two large pottery jars, planted with dwarf papyrus that shot up a good two cubits. The jars were elaborately painted in the Egyptian style, with colorful lotus flowers and geometric designs.

The Queen herself greeted him dressed in a fine linen robe with an embroidered stripe of purple. The Queen's hair was styled in an ornate knot on top of her head, secured with a bronze clip, and she had taken the time to put kohl around her eyes and rouge on her cheeks. Queen Donitaya evidently dressed up for his visit. Although he was a eunuch, Thut-Moses still felt flattered.

Gesturing for Thut-Moses to take one of the chairs, she sat down as well. The serving girl set out small tables, offering cheeses, olives, and watered-down red wine.

"And how did Gibor-El treat you?" Queen Donitaya asked. "That is his name, the guard downstairs. Quite a name, too-- 'Hero of the gods.'"

"He was pleasant enough," answered Thut-Moses.

The Queen continued, "He may appear gruff, but beneath that exterior lies a decent man. The children tease him relentlessly. He is captain of the King's Guard. An experienced soldier, having fought for the Hittites in their last war with the Kaska tribe. Beware crossing him, though, his spear skills are formidable. On his days off, a younger guard takes his place. But I feel safest when Gibor-El stands watch."

Thut-Moses took a sip of wine and nibbled on cheese. "I have met him before. I have heard that he is a fine soldier. I will try not to cross him.."

They started talking about the scroll the scribe had brought. He showed it to her and carefully unrolled it. The scroll was written on papyrus, in pen and ink, in hieratic script of Egypt. "This is a copy, of course," Thut-Moses said with a note of reverence in his voice. "The original scroll was written at least four hundred years ago. Copies have been made since then."

"You really are a scholar at heart," Queen Donatiya said. "Nothing makes you happier than reading ancient documents. Is it all right if I pick it up?"

Thut-Moses nodded his assent. The Queen carefully picked up the scroll and started examining it.

While she was distracted, Thut-Moses sat quietly and took in the opulent surroundings. His gaze traveled to a terrace overlooking the courtyard, with the pool and garden beyond. Doors remained ajar, allowing a gentle breeze to weave through the rooms.

The Queen gave him back the scroll.

"I cannot make any sense of it. Read it to me." Her friendly tone softened the command. Thut-Moses took back the scroll and started scanning it.

"The introduction says that this papyrus describes fifty-two patients. The physician's goal is to decide which of them he can certainly help; which are beyond help; and which he can try to help, without any guarantees of success.".

"The first five cases involve wounds to the head," Thut-Moses continued "This first case involves a poor fellow who has had his skull smashed in. You can see the brain material protruding from the wound. He can't use his arms or legs. His speech is nonsense. The wise physician decides that the patient is beyond help."

"I would have known that at first glance!" Queen Donitaya said. "Surely, he did not need to give us this case!"

"These physicians were nothing if not thorough," Thut-Moses replied. "They were military surgeons, attending to the men wounded on the battlefield. "

"Can you just summarize these cases? Or skip ahead to someone who can be treated? asked the Queen.

"I agree with you," said Thut-Moses. "We will look for those cases where the patient can be treated, if that is acceptable to her majesty."

"Here we go, fractures that can be treated!" Thut-Moses read to her how to treat broken bones, which was effective and did not involve undue death and dying.

Then he read about the surgical instruments. "One should use surgical instruments that have been thoroughly cleansed between one patient and the next. The knife should be washed and the put through the fire, to make sure it is clean."

"Egyptians are sticklers for cleanliness," Thut-Moses added. "They are that way with personal hygiene, certainly. The men shave daily because they cannot abide any body hair."

Celebrating the review of the scroll with another cup of wine, they arranged to meet again.

"Perhaps next time we can read something from the Ugaritic tales?" Queen Donatiya suggested "A story perhaps with a bit of mayhem, the gods interfering in the affairs of men? Those are always enlightening. Or entertaining at least."

Thut-Moses smiled. He agreed to return in one week with something more light-hearted than a medical scroll. He thought to himself: "Queen Donitaya would have made a fine ruler in her own right."

CHAPTER 8: OF GIANTS AND SEA MONSTERS

As the sun was dipping in the west, Menelaus returned to Yoninah's house for another meal. They sat down to eat dinner in the shade provided by an awning on the roof-terrace. His arm was healing nicely. The sling came off and he could use the arm again.

This dinner was a modest meal of barley, beans, lentils, and cheese, with fresh dates dipped in honey for dessert. After the meal, Bat-El and Laylah peppered him with questions. He had already told them he was Mycenean but hadn't been back for decades.

"Tell us more about Mycenae!" the girls demanded.

"Mycenae lies across the Sea," Menelaus stroked his beard. "The land has a grand palace, with a great wall around it. My father was a guard at the King's gate. One time, I remember, there was an earthquake. The walls collapsed. The city had to build them up again."

"I was still a boy back then. Our king, Agamemnon, asked for soldiers to go fight a war for him. I was looking for an adventure. So, I went to fight. A whole fleet of our boats went up against the city of Troy. We were there for a good ten years, which wasn't the adventure I wanted. Then I came to Ugarit, which I like well enough. I've been here twenty years."

"Have you heard any news from Mycenae, since you left?" Laylah asked.

"There are always stories, When the men gather at the taverns, they like to tell stories. I heard a story the other day. I don't know if it's true. This fellow, about my age, tells me he is from Mycenae. This was over several beers. He says he used to be a soldier at Troy, like I was. He had quite a story about what happened when they boarded their ships, to finally leave Troy and sail back home. Mind you, this was twenty years ago."

"This was a big man talking." Menelaus gestured with his hands to indicate the man's height. "He wasn't someone who looked like he scared easily. But the story he told was wild. The first day went fine, he said. They got on their ships, with

18 oarsmen each, with sails unfurled to catch the wind and started back to Mycenae. Then all sorts of mayhem happened."

"He said the ship got lost in a terrible storm, getting blown way off course. They came to an island and went ashore to find food and water. But the people who lived there were giants and attacked them and they lost a few men before getting back to their boat."

At this juncture, Bat-El voiced an appreciative "Giants?"

"Aye, that's what they said," said Menelaus.

"When they set out again, there was a giant sea creature. He said it had eight arms that were twenty cubits long! Coming out of the deep, it attacked the boat and sank it. A few men swam on the debris and saved themselves. He was one of them. The rest of the crew, a good forty men, they drowned."

"That's terrible!" Bat-El said, her eyes big as saucers.

"My storyteller, he survived for three days, afloat on a piece of wood, and came ashore in Cyprus. Some fishermen took him in and nursed him back to health. He decided to stay in Cyprus. He married a nice woman and all that and has three children now. "

"This fellow, he will sail along the east coast of the Great Sea. He sails from Cyprus to Ugarit and maybe to Acco. But he is not willing to head any further west than Cyprus, with the land of giants and the sea monsters out there. And, like I said, he's a big guy, strong and fierce looking. So, it wasn't a small thing that took away his courage."

Again, the youngsters and Yoninah were duly impressed. Although Yoninah harbored some doubts as to the exact details of this big man's misadventure.

****

After dinner and the storytelling, the young people went to bed. Yonina and Menelaus lingered over the last cup of wine.

"My daughters enjoy your stories," Yoninah said. "Thank you for keeping them entertained. You are quite the storyteller."

Touching her arm occasionally, they talked a bit more. The hour was growing late. A full moon had risen, and the stars were scattered across the night sky.

"I have to get back home." Menelaus cleared his throat.

"You can stay the night, if you like," Yoninah offered this with some hesitation. She was afraid he would say no.

"Best offer I've had in years." Menelaus' eyes crinkled when he smiled.

Later that night, as they lay entwined together in bed, Yoninah thought, "It has been a long time since I've had a handsome man in my bed. Or any man, for that matter."

Menelaus turned out to be a gentle and attentive lover. Afterwards, he ran his fingers through her dark hair.

"Your hair is lovely. And your skin is so smooth." Menelaus said softly.

Yoninah felt comforted. She thought maybe she was too old for lovemaking. Turns out, she was not. They fell asleep in each other's arms.

CHAPTER 9: STORY OF KIRTE

Thut-Moses and Queen Donitaya met again in the Queen's apartment. This time, they sat on her terrace, overlooking the courtyard below. Spring had arrived. The sun's rays shone gently on the stones of the courtyard, with colorful flowers blooming in ornate pots.

Last time they had met, the Queen had requested to read something more exciting than a medical papyrus from the Egyptians. She had asked for a story from the Ugaritic epics. The epics promised dramatic fighting between the gods and courtly dramas that played out on the celestial level.

A serving girl brought out tables for them and gave them cups of wine. Thut-Moses took out the scroll he had brought. This one was written in the Ugaritic script.

"I believe this will satisfy your desire for drama and excitement." Thut-Moses inclined his head to the Queen. He began reading in a resonant voice:

"This is the story of Kirte. He was the first king of Ugarit. His family – a wife and eleven children - - had all died. Four babies at birth, three of disease, two in accidents, one lost at sea, and one fallen into a water channel."

"It is true, many children die young. Although eleven seems excessive." The Queen interjected, her eyes sparkling with humor.

Thut-Moses acknowledged her comment and continued the story:

"Kirte wept for his lost children. He fell asleep. In a dream, El – his patron and perhaps his father—appeared. El saw his tears and offered him silver and gold and other treasures, to comfort him. "Why should I want silver and gold? Give me sons!" Kirte exclaimed.

"True for any king. He must have sons, he must have a successor.," the Queen opined.

"Kirte prayed to El, asking for more children," Thut-Moses stated. "El instructed him: "Offer sacrifices to the gods. Then gather an army and march seven days; besiege the kingdom of Udm, to gain the hand of the King's daughter Hurriah. Kirte followed these instructions. He marched for seven days to the city of Udm, and laid siege to the city. The king of Udm was overwhelmed by the mass of Kirte's army. He offered Kirte gold and silver and other prizes if he ended the siege and left the city alone. 'I have no need for gold and silver,' Kirte said. 'Give me the hand of your daughter Hurriah in marriage.' Thus, Kirte gained the hand of Hurriah, who was beautiful and gracious."

"Of course she is beautiful and gracious. In these stories, all the women are beautiful. Although not all are gracious," said the Queen. She took another sip of wine.

Thut-Moses continued: "El blessed Kirte's marriage. He and his wife went on to have seven daughters and two sons."

"Can you imagine? Nine children!" said the Queen. "Sounds exhausting."

"The story continues," said Thut-Moses. "Some years later, Kirte unfortunately angered one of the goddesses. He was stricken by disease and took to his bed. He was sick for four months. His family thought he was dying. There was drought in the land. If the king was sick, the land became fallow. Baal saw the land suffering – because the king was dying – and asked El the Compassionate to intervene...El made the figure of Stataqat the Healer out of clay. He sends her to expel the illness from Kirte."

"A healer made by the gods. That is wonderful," said the Queen. She leaned forward to hear the end of the tale.

"The Healer waved a wand and said the words that drive out the fever. Kirte regained his strength and his appetite and sat again on the throne. At this juncture, Yassub, his oldest son, came to speak with Kirte. Yassub chastised his father, saying: 'When raiders raid, you talk. When there are invaders, you are idle. You do not judge the cases of widows. You do not preside over the hearings of the oppressed. Instead, you languish on a bed of disease.'"

"It's true. The King has a duty to protect the kingdom, to protect the widows and orphans, to render judgments that are fair. The boy has made a good argument. Except the King has regained his strength, so it does not pertain," judiciously noted the Queen.

"Yassub threatened to oust Kirte from the throne." said the scribe. "Kirte, who was strong again, put curses on the head of Yassub and drove him from his presence."

"That seems about right! The King cannot allow a son to usurp the throne like that," said the Queen. "It happens all too often, at least among the Hittites and the Egyptians." She looked out the window towards the foreign lands.

****

After Thut-Moses finished the tale, they drank their cups of wine in companionable silence.

"I enjoyed that story." The Queen graced Thut-Moses with a smile.

In turn, Thut-Moses thanked her for her insightful commentary. He did enjoy spending time with Queen Donitaya.

As a eunuch, Thut-Moses knew he had unique access to the Queen's apartment. He would never be allowed a friendship with the Queen otherwise.

"Perhaps we can meet again next week?" Thut-Moses asked. "How about a story of the gods fighting with each other? That is always amusing."

Queen Donitaya happily agreed to meet again. She enjoyed Thut-Moses' company, although she did occasionally think it was a shame he would never father children of his own. The intelligent and handsome Thut-Moses would have made a splendid father, she thought to herself. However, the Queen was wise enough not to share that thought with her husband.

****

They would have to meet while mild days of spring persisted and before the summer heat drove Queen Donitaya and the other royals from the city. The royal family always went to the mountains for the summer months.

CHAPTER 10: IN THE HEAT OF SUMMER

At the Healer's House

As summer swept through the city, with the fruit trees in nearby orchards in full bloom, Menelaus moved into Yoninah's house. The rooms on the upper level were getting too hot from the heat of the summer sun. They all slept on the roof terrace now, for the sake of the cool nighttime breezes. The girls slept on one side of the roof terrace, on their sleeping mats. Yoninah and Menelaus slept on the opposite side of the roof. The roof-terrace was supplied with a half-wall, to keep one from falling off. It also had a thatch-covered shelter at one side, to provide shade as needed or in case of rain. Which was sparse in the summer.

There was a new rhythm to their days. When she woke up in the morning, Yoninah enjoyed the solid comfort of his body next to hers. She would run her fingers down his back: the skin was smooth and firm in an interesting shade of olive, perhaps a smidgeon lighter than her own.

In the morning, he would take bread and cheese for breakfast and then he would leave for the harbor. Welcoming him back home in the evening, they would share a meal with the girls. Sometimes he brought back figs and dates, which were always welcome additions to their larder. Yoninah would tell stories from her day about patients who had come to her healer's shop. Menelaus would share the stories he heard in the harbor.

The younger people would listen eagerly to these stories, especially if they involved the gods, giants, or monsters. At this dinner, not only Bat-El and Laylah were listening to Menelaus' tales, but also Gedalyah – the boy from next door, Bat-El's friend. He was also ten years old. Very pleased with himself: he had just started at the school for scribes. A great honor, as he let them know incessantly.

"Today, I heard a story from a group of sailors from Acco," Menelaus said. "It's about giants who walk the land. Do you want to hear it?" he asked the young people.

Gedalyah's eyes grew big. He especially liked stories about giants. And monsters. "Oh yes, tell us!" he said.

"All right," said Menelaus. "The folk from Acco, they have the same gods as in Ugarit. They say their gods are mighty and tall and walk with giant steps across the earth. These gods sometimes have children with human women. Only the most beautiful of the human women, of course. And the children are always tall. Not as tall as the gods but much taller than ordinary men. And they grow up to be great heroes, with the strength of ten."

Menelaus continued: "These 'Rephaim'(as they call them) are said to do mighty deeds. They kill great sea monsters, the Leviathans. They fight in mortal conflicts, when their human relatives go to battle against their enemies."

"Are these stories, are they true?" asked Bat-El.

"The men from Acco swear on the existence of these giants," replied Menelaus. "They know about them because of the great bones they leave, buried in the ground. They say they find leg bones that are five or six cubits long. Five cubits would make for a very tall man. These people must have been at least two heads taller than me, and I am a tall man...."

"Have you ever seen one of the Rephaim?" asked Gedalyah.

"No," answered Menelaus. "But we Myceneans, we too have stories of half-gods. We call them 'demigods" or 'halflings'. Hercules is the most famous. He was a true hero. He carried out feats of impossible strength. He was the son of Zeus and a human mother. I do not know if these stories are true or not. But the sailors swear by them."

Yoninah was smiling during this exchange. She found Menelaus' stories a perennial source of amusement.

****

At another dinner, Menelaus brought presents for the girls. He gave Bat-El a small terra cotta figure of a camel.

"I got this from a trader who bought it in Arabia," he told her. "This trader, he says they use camels to carry goods across the Arabian desert. What an odd-looking creature, don't you think? But he says they can carry ten times as much as a donkey and they can take the heat of the desert, and they do not need water to drink because they store their water in their hump. See the hump?"

Fascinated by this odd-looking animal, Bat-El adopted it and added it to her menagerie of exotic creatures. She already had the figure of an elephant as a keepsake from her father, the captain, who had brought it back for her after one of his trips.

For Laylah, he had a small terra-cotta jar, painted with red and black designs.

"This too I got from the trader from Arabia," he said. "Here, open it! It contains a fine perfume made from the flowers of jasmine."

Laylah was also captivated by her gift. She and added it to her collection of jars in which she kept her kohl and other treasures.

****

On a clear night that summer, with the stars shining brightly across the swathe of the sky, with a full moon rising in the east, Menelaus and Yoninah set up their sleeping mats on the rooftop terrace. The days were getting hot, and the nights stayed hot as well. As they enjoyed the cool of the evening breezes. they felt a tremor. The house shook for the space of three breaths and then returned to its normal parameters.

"They're never strong, these tremors," Menelaus said. "Perhaps a crack in the plaster, is all. They have been coming more often lately. Nothing like the earthquakes we saw in Mycenae."

Yoninah was no fool and was not easily reassured about the import of tremors in Ugarit. She had heard about an earthquake that occurred when her mother was young and had taken down some of the walls in Ugarit. She was pleased though that Menelaus sought to comfort her with his gentle interpretation of the significance of tremors.

They settled peaceably into their mats and blankets. After the girls had fallen asleep, Yoninah told Menelaus about the captain and the loss of her baby five years before.

"When the captain died, it was a terrible time for me," she said. "When I heard that his ship sank, I was pregnant, already big with child. The child would kick me all the time before then. When they told me the captain wasn't coming back, I fainted. Never did that before. The baby wasn't kicking after that. I went into labor the next day."

Yoninah's voice caught in her throat. She had rarely spoken of that day.

"It was a boy," Yoninah said softly. "The cord wrapped around his neck. He was dead. This was a double loss for me. The captain, then the child."

Menelaus wrapped his arm around her and gave her a gentle squeeze.

"After the birth, I ran a high fever. I was in a fever-dream for a week. Bright colors, lots of flying. Vivid images where I would go looking for the captain or go looking for the new baby…When I came through the fevers, the midwife came and told me that I was lucky to be alive, but that I would have no more pregnancies. I accepted this without question. My husband was gone. I was not anticipating any more children."

"Were you better by then, after the fever broke?" asked Menelaus.

"No, it took months to get better," Yoninah said. " I went into a dark place. I had no desire to get out of bed. As the prophets say, an evil spirit came over me…I wanted to die. Nothing gave me pleasure. I didn't want to eat, only to sleep. To join my husband and son in the afterworld."

"I am so sorry to hear that," murmured Menelaus.

"My mother was alive then. She took care of me. She brought me soup or stews to sip, beer to drink. She was insistent that I take some nourishment. So, I did."

Yoninah fell silent for a moment. "It took awhile until I got better., three or four months. My daughter Layla helped me.

She was only ten that year. She would rub my hands and sing to me when I took to my bed, which I did a lot. She had lost her father. She said she didn't want to lose her mother too. A sweet child. Her little sister was only five. She would come visit me also. She became Laylah's little shadow, during those months."

"Then what happened?" Menelaus sensed she wasn't done with her story.

"One morning I woke up and could hear the birds sing and feel the gentle rays of sun on my face." Yoninah touched her face as if she could still feel the sun's warmth. "I thought, 'Bat-El would like barley grain soaked in goat milk for breakfast.' I got up and made her breakfast. And then I took up the other pieces of my life as well. I could enjoy food again and gained some weight. And then I started working again."

"Was it hard to go back to work as a healer?" asked Menelaus.

"It was a pleasure to go back to work. I found I had gained patience with my clients," Yoninah said. "Many of them were in distress. Why else see a healer? No one comes to see me because they feel good. No, they're always in pain. Either physical pain or in their hearts. The physical is easy to treat.

Give them salves or teas with poppy extract. The pain in the heart is not so easy to treat."

"They too would have lost a child," Yoninah continued. "Or a husband gone astray with another woman. The stories I heard were heartrending. But I would listen, which was a salve itself. I knew what that felt like, to lose a child or a husband gone missing. I could tell them to use this prayer or that amulet and the pain would eventually pass. I could say this with the conviction of someone who had experienced it myself."

"You are a good listener," Menelaus said encouragingly.

"Although it never goes away completely, the heartache. I still talk to the captain, at times. I know he is in the afterlife."

"Should I be jealous?" Menelaus said, but in a teasing tone of voice.

"We Ugaritics have tombs below the courtyard of the house, off to one side, with a staircase going down. For my husband, I set up a shrine since his body was lost at sea. I bring him red wine. I tell him how the girls are growing up. I still talk to my son, in the tombs below. I want him to know that I still grieve for him and for the child I never watched grow up. But the grief is bearable now and no longer crippling."

Menelaus listened patiently to this tale and treated her even more gently thereafter.

Chapter 11: BAAL'S BATTLE WITH SEA

Thut-Moses and Queen Donitaya met again in the palace for their literary adventures. This time, they sat in the pavilion in the courtyard. It provided a roof overhead to protect them from the summer sun.

Off to one side of the pavilion was a garden, with trees of olives and flowering shrubs. Twenty paces away, a fountain gurgled its way down a stone wall to fill the Egyptian style pool. The sound of trickling water made for a relaxing backdrop. A mother duck and her six ducklings swam in the pool's waters. The temperatures were pleasant enough in the late morning, especially with the shade provided in the pavilion.

"What have you brought to read this time?" Queen Donitaya asked. "Something Ugaritic, with a smattering of violence and gods fighting with each other, by any chance?"

Before Thut-Moses can answer, they were interrupted by the Queen's young servant girl, with smooth brown arms and legs flashing in the sun. She deposited a tray of cheese and fruit on small tables nearby.

"You are right," Thut-Moses said. "This is indeed a story about a battle between the gods."

"These stories remind me of quarrels inside the royal palace." The Queen waved her hand to indicate the interior of the palace. "One brother angry with another, waiting for the king to get old or die. Everyone competing for the throne."

"These stories *are* about quarrels inside a palace," Thut-Moses said. "Albeit a celestial palace, not an earthly one. One brother fighting with another, with the aging king watching from the sidelines."

Thut-Moses nibbled on a piece of cheese before starting the tale: "In this story, Baal – one of the younger gods –gets into a quarrel with Sea, a fellow-god. Sea has power over the seas and rivers. The king in this celestial family is El. He is the oldest of the gods and the father of the gods. Asherah is the Mother Goddess. She is called the 'Queen of Heaven.' She often tells El what to do. But that is another story."

"Queens often tell their Kings what to do," the Queen observed.

Thut -Moses continued: "Baal is jealous because Sea had gotten himself a palace on Mount Saphon. That is where the gods live. And Baal has no palace. Without a palace, Baal has no power. So, of course, they will battle with each other. The craftsman god -- his name is Kothar --favors Baal over Sea and gives him two magical clubs. With these magical clubs, Baal can strike Sea effectively. Baal strikes Sea twice on the skull. Sea stumbles and dies. The other gods proclaim: "Sea is dead. May Baal reign! May Baal gain his own house on Mount Saphon!"

"Do you read this story to children?" Queen Donitaya asked. "Do they get scared when one god is smashing another to pieces?"

"Yes, I have read this story to children, in the scribal school," Thut-Moses said. "They very much enjoy the brutality. They act out the parts. One child pretends to strike another, and the second child collapses to the ground, and a third child proclaims the victory of Baal over Sea. The children quite enjoy this part."

"The next chapter is about Anat," Thut-Moses said. "She is Baal's sister. A powerful goddess in her own right. She can cross a thousand fields with one step. She has a fierce temper. She loves Baal with all her heart and will do anything to protect him. She goes to El in his house on Mount Saphon, to ask him to provide a house for Baal. She actually threatens to smash El's head if he doesn't build a palace for Baal. El agrees to send Kothar to build a fine house for Baal, on Mount Saphon."

"Anat speaks like that, to the father of the gods?" Queen Donitaya said. "She is powerful enough to intimidate El? We have no such stories in Amurru."

Thut-Moses picked up the story: "The house that Kothar builds is beautiful, with cedars of Laebanon, gold, silver, and lapis lazuli. The walls are made of finely worked stone, covered with plaster and painted red. There are statues of gold and a grand staircase going up. There are windows for the sun to come though. There are courtyards, fountains, pools, and gardens.

"Sounds lovely," said the Queen. "Sounds just like our palace, here in Ugarit."

Thut-Moses continuesd: "Once he has bested Sea in battle and has built a grand palace on Mount Saphon, Baal comes into his full powers. Now he becomes Baal the Conqueror, Rider of the Clouds. He controls the rain and ensures that the land is watered, that the wheat and barley and trees grow in their season. "

"Are there many stories about Baal?" asks the Queen.

"Of course. In these stories, we see that Baal is strong. He wins many battles. He is the protector of Ugarit. "

"Well, I hope he keeps our enemies far away," the Queen said with a note of skepticism in her voice. "I prefer strong city walls manned by a phalanx of armed soldiers. But a strong celestial protector is also good."

Thut-Moses smiled at the Queen's cynicism. They talked some more about Anat.

"There is another story about Anat," said Thut-Moses. "In this story, she single-handedly battles human enemies on the earthly plane. She strikes them down with her sword. Severed heads roll under her like balls. She ties the heads to her belt and then wades knee-deep in soldiers' blood…then she washes off the blood and beautifies herself with murex."

"How unpleasant," said the Queen. "And impressive at the same time. Let us have a cup of wine, to finish the day. Mistress Anat stories make me want to drink wine. Not sure what to make of her."

"Anat reminds me of 'Sekhment' from Egypt," Thut-Moses said as he swirled the wine around in his cup. "She is the goddess of war. She also relishes bloodshed and is feared by the other gods."

And so the two friends finished their literary session with wine. The children came outside with their royal tutors and scampered in the pool. The day's heat made a dip in a cold pool an excellent idea.

The Queen's eleven-year-old son came over to his mother. "What did you read today?" She smiled at him and tousled his hair. He was a handsome young man.

"A story about the gods fighting. It has lots of blood and gore. Do you want me to tell it to you later?"

"Of course!" He smiled broadly and off he ran to rejoin the other children in the pool.

Thut-Moses and Queen Donitaya arranged to meet for another time. "If the gods are willing," they said. The sun went behind a cloud at this point. Perhaps a celestial omen, thought Thut-Moses. But he said nothing.

CHAPTER 12: BAD DREAMS

Menelaus

As the summer heat continued to besiege the city, Yoninah and Menelaus began sleeping routinely on the rooftop terrace. It offered a welcome reprieve from the heat.

Menelaus' sleep, however, was often disturbed by nightmares. In the middle of the night, he would thrash and turn and even shout out. Yoninah would wake him fully and reassure him that it had been a dream, nothing more. With luck, he would go back to sleep and not have another dream filled with terrors.

In her healer's shop, Yoninah had talked to retired military men whose wives brought them to see her.

"He has nightmares," the wives said. "They are always about the war. Can you give him something to take these evil dreams away?"

Yoninah would give them Valerian tea or some other sleeping draught.

After Menelaus had woken her up for five or six nights with such a dream, she couldn't help prying the next morning.

"Are these bad dreams about the war?" Yoninah asked.

"Yes, they are about the war," Menelaus scrubbed his face. "I was just a boy when I decided to go off to war. I was not prepared for the bloodshed and mayhem. "

Yoninah laid a comforting hand on his arm. "No one is ever prepared, I think."

"We won an engagement, the next time the Trojans won," Menelaus said. "It was a stalemate. We were there, camped on their shore, for ten years. We lost many men. So did they. Their walls were impregnable."

"Ten years, camped on a beach?" Yoninah asked.

"Somehow we tricked them and got through their gates. And took their gold and silver, ravaged the city, burnt it to the ground, took the women hostage, and killed the men. Children left crying in the streets. Did not leave a good taste in my mouth, to see all that slaughter. But that is the nature of war. The cities back home also suffered during those ten years that the men were away. More predators lurked around the great walls surrounding Mycenae and Pylos. Everyone paid a price for the war."

He paused for a moment. She was at a loss as to what words of comfort she could offer.

"I still have bad dreams from the war," Menelaus said. "My friends getting killed in Troy, the cries of Trojan women for their slaughtered children. All of it takes a toll on a man."

Another pause, a bit longer this time.

"The bad dreams are about the war," he continued. "And no, I don't want any sleep draught. I know how your mind works. The dreams are less frequent now. It's been a good twenty years since the war was over. I am doing fine now."

That was the end of that conversation, thought Yoninah to herself. She filed this conversation away and respected Menelaus' reticence to continue it any further. So typical for a man, to refuse help.

****

The King's Dreams

Meanwhile, the King was also having bad dreams.

A week earlier, King Ammurabi had gotten word of a mad prophet in the street who was making the people anxious with his talk of imminent doom. The King's weasel-faced advisor had told him of the man, and the disturbing words of his prophecy. Accordingly, the man had been arrested and put into jail. Then the King started having bad dreams, as if the words of the mad prophet had somehow crept into his dreamscape.

The same nightmare tormented the King three nights in a row. In his dream, he saw the birds covering the bright courtyard. Then a great wind blew, and the sky grew dark. The birds fell from the sky in a terrifying sight. The children had been in the courtyard playing, but they started screaming when the birds dropped to the earth. Then the earth shook with a low rumble.

"Run, Ammurabi! Seek shelter for yourself and your children!" a voice thundered from the sky.

In the dream, the King did not hesitate. He obeyed the voice from the sky and grabbed his wives and children and ran for the shelter of the palace walls.

In his dream-vision, the royal family gained the shelter of the palace. The King thought they were safe. But then he saw the figure of the mad prophet, his bright sharp eyes and his left hand holding fire. The King smelled fire up ahead, further along the hall. The prophet opened a door the King hadn't noticed before.

"Go through here!" the prophet commanded.

On the other side of the dream-door, the King and his family found themselves in a strange land. They were no longer in Ugarit. He was suddenly afraid. Had all his children come through the door? Were they all safe? He started calling out their names. And woke up, with dread in his heart.

He called for Thut-Moses who came quickly, even though it was the middle of the night. He asked Thut-Moses to listen to his dream and to write it down.

"If we fail to record it quickly, the dream vision will quickly evaporate." The King's face was still pale.

After Thut-Moses had recorded the dream, the King motioned for a glass of water.

"I am afraid it is sent by the gods. An oracle. What do you think?" The King asked his scribe.

"The sky growing dark, that is from the day that the sun disappeared," "Thut-Moses said in his most reassuring voice. "The prophecy of wind, earthquake, and fire…that is from the words of the mad prophet, the one with the wild gray hair and beard."

The King nodded as color slowly returned to his face.

"Should I send for him?" Thut-Moses asked. "The prophet is in the dungeon, as you know. Perhaps he was more skilled at prophecy than we thought."

"Yes, send for him." The King waved a hand. "Perhaps this would be a good time to let him leave the city, as a form of recompense. And to keep him from scaring the people of the city. I do not want the people to know I have had this dream. We will offer sacrifices to the gods and libations. And hopefully, the dream will prove to be no more than a fleeting indigestion."

And so the wild-eyed prophet was released from the dungeon that very night and told to leave the city and not to return. And the chief priest at the Temple was apprised of an enhanced schedule of sacrifices from the Temple altars. And the King was able to go back to sleep. Although Thut-Moses had a difficult night. The King's dream-visions had struck a deep chord in his heart. Sleep eluded him for the remainder of the night.

CHAPTER 13: Tahir's Arrival at the Healer's House

As the sun dropped low on the horizon, the daytime heat finally dissipating, Yoninah heard a firm knock at the door to the street. She opened the door and there stood a young man.

"You must be Tahir," she said. "Menelaus speaks highly of you."

The youth had the hazel eyes native to the mountainous tribes of Afghanistan. As he acknowledged his identity and crossed the threshold, Yoninah noticed that he moved with the grace of a natural athlete. Like the Ugaritic, his complexion was olive in color. His face was handsome enough and clean shaven, but Yoninah noticed he was a head shorter than Menelaus.

Tahir greeted Menelaus warmly and thanked Yoninah, as the woman of the house, for inviting him to dinner. Tahir wore a fine wool tunic and sported a gold necklace and gold earrings to match.

Yoninah introduced him to Bat-El, her younger daughter. He greeted her appropriately, with a smile and a brief nod of his head. Then she introduced Laylah, the fifteen-year-old. Laylah was a startlingly pretty girl, with dark eyes and black hair and a face of unusual symmetry and gentle lines. Tahir seemed happy to have someone close to his own age as company. His eyes rested on her longer than was strictly necessary.

Yoninah could tell, however, that Laylah was not that impressed. She was busy having crushes on all the sailors who came through the port and into town. Her mother knew that Laylah liked the boys that were tall, the Ethiopians or the Myceneans or the ones from the Caucasus. Although Laylah did compliment Tahir on his fine gold jewelry.

They sat down to dinner on the terrace, for the sake of the evening breezes, with a low table placed before them. They sat cross-legged on mats around the table to enjoy a dinner of mutton. A neighbor had slaughtered a sheep and given Yoninah the meat in exchange for a bronze amulet.

Tahir held court. He spoke with a faint accent, with added guttural inflections to his vowels. Tahir had a way with words, and Menelaus let him monopolize the conversation on this first visit.

"Tell them about how you came to be in Ugarit," Menelaus told him.

Tahir launched into the tale of his origins. He was born in a town in Afghanistan and his mother died when he was ten. He never knew his father. Homeless for two years, he stole food and other things to survive. The city guards caught him stealing.

"Either you go to jail, or you join the donkey caravans," the guards told twelve-year-old Tahir. Tahir joined the caravans.

Tahir tended the donkeys. Already as strong as a grown man despite his short stature, he could load up the goods quickly. He lifted tin ingots from the Afghani mountains and bags of poppy seeds from the countryside. Tahir also loaded the lapis lazuli and elephant ivory.

Tahir worked the caravans for three years. He learned to handle a spear and dagger. The donkey caravans were attacked every so often, as they crossed the hundred-day distance, along the Highway from Afghanistan to Mari, from which secondary caravans would carry the goods to the Great Sea.

"Tell them about the attack on the caravan!" interjected Menelaus.

Tahir launched into a story of an attack on their camp by some heavily armed brigands.

"There was a midnight attack on our camp," Tahir's gold necklace winked in the waning light. "We were asleep in the tent, with the sentry keeping watch at the tent door. The fellow on the watch had drunk too much beer and had fallen asleep on the job. There were bandits on the road, always trying to steal donkeys loaded up with cargo."

"Wouldn't you hear the donkeys?" Laylah asked.

"I heard a commotion outside the tent, which woke me up," Tahir said. "I picked up my lance and looked out the tent flap to see what was going on. Big mistake. Someone hit me hard on the head – maybe a fist, maybe a lance – and knocked me out. When I came to, I saw that everyone else was either dead or unconscious. The donkeys and cargo were gone."

"How awful!" Laylah said.

"There were three of us who survived. We made our way to the relative safety of Mari. From there, I joined a caravan going to Ugarit. Never went back to the caravans."

"Then what happened?" asked Laylah.

"Why, I like Ugarit. It's a lively town. I found work on the docks. Been here now for two, almost three years. I have a room near the harbor. I have a dog who keeps me company. And Menelaus here, who listens to my stories and tells a few of his own…I can bring my dog with me, if I come again for dinner."

Yoninah and the girls were duly impressed by his story of the attack on the caravan and his journey to Ugarit. Although Yoninah did question its veracity. She knew that sailors and other young men often made up tales to impress girls.

There were yet more stories and more glasses of wine. Tahir told them how he made extra money by buying and selling goods smuggled ashore by the sailors. He used the money to buy the gold jewelry he proudly displayed.

As the hour grew late, Yoninah offered to make up a rough bed for Tahir in the courtyard. It was late at night, and the streets were not always safe at night. Plus the tale of brigands made her nervous. The night sky was clear: no risk of their guest getting rained on in the courtyard.

Yoninah did ask the girls to latch their door. She was not entirely certain of the young man's intentions. He was gone by morning when he had to be back at the harbor.

Yoninah invited Tahir again. The next time, he brought his dog, an Afghan hound. The well-behaved dog sat patiently at Tahir's side during dinner. He fed her scraps under the table.

Tahir and the dog would appear every seventh night, when they routinely ate a good meal. Bat-El would sit with the dog at every visit and pet the hound endlessly. Both Bat-El and the dog seemed to enjoy it.

****

At the next dinner they shared, Laylah teased Tahir about being soft-hearted when it came to his dog. She said, "You take such good care of her. You keep her groomed. She always appears clean and happy."

"She is smart and a good companion," Tahir said. "She is loyal. Dogs do not abandon you. They do not talk and speak foolishness like some people."

Yoninah was listening to this exchange. She wondered if Tahir counted Laylah as one of the foolish people. If so, he did so at his own peril, she thought.

Laylah paused for a second. She skipped over his would-be insult and pressed on with her questions.

"Did you have a dog in Afghanistan?" she asked.

"No, not in Afghanistan," Tahir gave the dog an affectionate scratch behind the ears. "Only when I started working in the caravans, then there were dogs. This one is a Tazi hound, the same as we had in the caravans. They were trained to protect the donkeys and the men and the cargo as we traveled through mountains and deserts. I grew fond of dogs. This dog was a puppy when I found her, wandering the streets of the docks, looking skinny and hungry. I shared my dinner with her, and she followed me home."

"You are soft-hearted," Laylah teased him.

Yoninah got up to clear the table. As she turned towards the kitchen, she heard Tahir say, "I am soft hearted when it comes to women, too, But I'm not going to tell you about that stuff."

Yoninah smiled as she listened to the two young people banter.

She saw Laylah get quiet and a blush steal over her cheeks. Her mother thought she acted like she was a bit jealous about these other women. She saw Laylah flip her long hair in an age-old gesture of "I'm a young woman with lovely hair, which I want you to notice as I dismiss you from my presence" as she turned away from Tahir and went to help Yoninah in the kitchen.

CHAPTER 14: TRADE AND DIPLOMACY IN UGARIT

On a fine summer day, with the trees thick with leaves and the flowers in full bloom, the King sent Thut-Moses on a mission.

Every month, Thut-Moses would go to the house of Urtenu, head merchant of Ugarit. Urtenu was an important man. He had advised the previous king for twenty years. Now he advised King Ammurabi. And collected taxes and fees for him.

The city was at the crossroads of trade routes. Goods from Mesopotamia to the east arrived by donkey caravan. Grain and gold from Egypt came in by ship, as did copper from Cyprus and fine pottery from Mycenae. The harbor became busy in early spring, when the winds were favorable for travel across the eastern Great Sea.

Ships coming into the harbor had to pay a fee for docking. They had to pay taxes based on the value of the cargo they carried. Similar fees and taxes obtained for land caravans as well. It ended up being a lot of silver and gold for the privilege of moving trade through the city.

The flow of gold and silver had made the kingdom wealthy. And had made Urtenu wealthy as well.

The merchant lived in a fine house, not far from the palace compound. On an upper floor of the house was a library of thousands of clay tablets. These recorded the trade contracts for the ships and caravans that came and went from Ugarit. As well as correspondences from kings along the margins of the Great Sea.

As Thut-Moses knocked on the stately front door, a servant answered and led him into the front room. Urtenu stood to greet him. The great man was dressed in the finest of tunics, with ornamental stripes of the prized purple thread. Urtenu wore heavy good chains on his neck, which distracted only a little from his large stomach. Clearly, Urtenu never passed up a fine meal of meat and red wine.

On this occasion, Thut-Moses noticed that the man walked with a limp. From conversations with the court physician, the eunuch knew Urtenu suffered from gout, a disease common with the elite facing the hazards of too rich a diet.

Thut-Moses thought Urtenu was pretentious and too fond of the sound of his own voice. Urtenu often offered opinions even if never asked. Although occasionally his opinions were valuable. Just occasionally.

The merchant had a close relationship with the Hittites. He had offices in Carchemesh, a Hittite city-state a seven-day distance by foot from Ugarit. From these offices, Urtenu had messengers coming and going to Ugarit and back again, regularly receiving communications from the Hittites. As a prominent merchant, Urtenu even received messages from Suppiluliuma, king of the Hittites.

On this visit, the two men exchanged the usual courtesies.

"I hope things are well with you and the King," Urtenu said politely.

"I hope you and your family are also well." Thut-Moses inclined his head.

Urtenu started by boasting that he had received a letter from the Pharoah himself.

"Egypt is happy with the shipments they have received, of copper from Cyprus, of tin from Afghanistan. Of course they are happy." Urtenu rested his hands on his large stomach.

"They will use these metals to good advantage, to make fine bronze weapons and chariots for Pharoah."

Urtenu also reported on two recent letters from Carchemesh.

"King Suppiluliuma still complains of drought and famine in his lands," Urtenu said. "He is again asking for shipments of grain from the storehouses in Egypt."

"Has the grain been sent?" Thut-Moses asked.

"One ship full of grain has already been dispatched to Hittite lands, and a second one is getting readied."

"Famine to the north, in Hittite lands, is worrisome," Urtenu continued. "Although drought happens with some regularity. With luck, the rains will return, and the crops will grow again."

There was a third letter from the court of the Hittites that he wanted to discuss with Thut-Moses.

"It is a bit puzzling," Urtenu said. Thut-Moses hid his surprise. Urtenu didn't usually admit to being puzzled.

Urtenu sent for his scribe Jeru-Baal, asking him to find the most recent clay tablet from Carchemesh in the library. Jeru-Baal was a slender young man, looking a bit harried. Perhaps Urtenu worked him too hard, thought Thut-Moses.

As they continued to wait for the scribe's return, Urtenu felt obligated to share with Thut-Moses his opinion of the Hittites.

"The once-mighty Hittites are faltering," Urtenu said. "They used to be a great power in the region. But they spent all their money and their soldiers fighting the Battle of Kadesh, some eighty years ago. Their confrontation with Egypt depleted their treasury. By the gods, it weakened both combatants. Neither side is as strong as before."

"I thought Ugarit and other vassal kingdoms send ample tribute to our Hittites overlords every year," said Thut-Moses." Surely their treasuries are augmented by now?"

"Apparently, not augmented enough, from what I have heard," said Urtenu.

Urtenu paused a short while, apparently lost in thought.

"One hopes our tithes and those of their other holdings suffice. But I am not entirely certain that the Hittites remain strong enough to keep up their end of the bargain, the part where their army protects our interests in the event of an attack," Urtenu concluded.

The scribe Jeru-Baal finally reappeared, holding a clay tablet. He carefully unwrapped it and started to translate it from Akkadian to Ugaritic.

From the king of the Hittites to Urtenu:

"What does Urtenu know of an Ugaritic seaman named Ibnadushu who was captured by foreigners in the Aegean Sea? These people live on ships. They are from Shekelesh. This Ibnadushu spent some time onboard the foreigners' ship and had gotten free at some point. And returned to Ugarit. I want to interview this person. I want to question him regarding the land of Shekelesh. I want him sent to Khatta so he could tell me what he knows. King Ammurabi is too young. He does not know much."

Urtenu laughed when the scribe got to the part about King Ammurabi's youth and lack of knowledge.

Thut-Moses, however, was not amused. Thut-Moses asked Urtenu if he should share this tablet with the King.

"I don't think I want to share the Hittite's actual words with our young king. I will send out men to find this Ibnadushu," Urtenus said. "If we find him, probably getting drunk in the harbor bars, then we can discuss it with King Ammurabi."

Thut-Moses hastily agreed to this plan of action.

****

When Thut-Moses returned to the palace, he reported to the King the news of continued drought and famine in the north. That grain from Egypt was being sent to remedy the situation.

"On a separate matter," he reported. "There is a report of a sailor from Ugarit who was held captive by foreigners and lived on their ship," Thut-Moses said. "This man was set free and likely headed back to Ugarit. King Suppiluliuma wants the man to be sent back to his court, so he can interview him. Urtenu is sending out men to find him."

The King did not know what to make of this odd story. Thut-Moses agreed it was a puzzling bit of information but not necessarily alarming.

The King returned to the other matters discussed with Urtenu. Thut-Moses shared the reports that the seaports remained busy, trade was brisk, and the royal treasury looked solid.

CHAPTER 15: The Baal Festival

At the house on Palace Street, Bat-El and Laylah wanted to go to the Baal Festival. Yoninah said that she would take them to the festival, as long as Tahir accompanied them. She wanted the extra security he provided. Too many young men there, too much wine, she thought.

Tahir agreed to go with them as a chaperone.

"I am not a Baal worshipper," Tahir confessed. "Is that a problem? He is one of your gods. I understand. But they are not my gods, not the gods of my people in Afghanistan."

"Just go with us and enjoy the music and the dancing," Yoninah said. "But help me keep an eye on my daughters! So don't enjoy the music and dancing too much. Or the wine too much."

The four of them went together. This was Bat-El's first time at the festival. She wore a new tunic with an embroidered blue stripe. Her hair was tied back with a blue ribbon. Bat-El's black eyes glowed with excitement. The blue accented the blackness of her hair, and even Laylah complimented her outfit.

Laylah was also wearing a new tunic of the finest linen. She had gold rings in her ears, and gold bracelets on her arms. The gold contrasted nicely with her olive skin.

Even Tahir was dressed up, wearing an embroidered tunic. With a gold chain on his neck and gold earrings, he looked like a rich man with inexplicable muscles. Lifting at the docks had made him strong, especially his arms.

Yoninah wore her favorite linen tunic and her finest bronze clasp on her shoulder. Her hair was braided and adorned with a matching clasp; her necklace of Asherah on full display on her chest.

Yoninah and the three young people climbed along Palace Street to the highest point in the city to the Temple Mount. Bat-El and Laylah quickened their steps as they heard the drums playing. As they approached Temple Mount, Yoninah could smell the heavy scent of cannabis and frankincense, burning in incense altars.

Crossing the ornate gates that led into the Temple compound, they saw the hulking figures of Hittite lions guarding it.

"A gift from our Hittite overlords," said Yoninah. She did not much care for Hittite statuary. She much preferred the more refined statues from their previous overlords, the Egyptians.

They saw hundreds of people—mostly young-- crowded into the grand plaza just inside the gates. As dusk fell, temple servants lit score of torches scattered throughout the plaza. The dancing flames added a note of magic to the scene.

"Look, look!" said Bat-El as she pointed to the figure of a man inscribed on a stele at the north end of the plaza. Bat-El was impressed by the life-sized figure cut into the stone face. He stood with a thunderbolt in one hand, his other hand holding a spear that seemed to be sprouting leaves at one end.

"That is Baal, the god of rain," said Yoninah. "His favor grants us the rain and with it, a good harvest. This spring has been a bit drier than usual, and the rivers are running lower than usual. The prayers and offerings to Baal will be heartfelt this year."

In front of them stood the Temple of Baal, a grand building with an imposing tower. Rising a good twenty cubits above the Temple itself, the tower provided an excellent view of the harbor and surrounding landscape.

Tahir said, "The men in the harbor talk about this Tower. At its top, a fire is kept burning throughout the night. Ships at sea can see the fire and know how far they are from the coast. They use the fire signal to guide their ships. Grateful ships' captains have given anchors as offerings to the Temple. Bat-El said, "I can see them! Four or five giant stone anchors are in the courtyard."

Across the plaza stood the entrance to the Temple. A majestic flight of stairs, with twenty finely finished stone steps, led up to the portico of the building. The portico itself was a grand structure, its roof held aloft with four great columns painted red. The portico led into the massive wooden doors of the temple.

From the doors, the onlookers saw three men emerge holding rams' horns. Standing on the portico, they lifted their instruments in unison and sounded three long blasts, which drew the attention of the mass of people standing on the plaza below. All eyes turned to the spectacle unfolding on the portico.

The figure of the High Priest appeared. He stood over the crowd: a tall, handsome man, dressed in a tunic decorated with a purple stripe. The High Priest wore heavy gold chains around his neck, with golden bells along the hem of his garment. He easily commanded attention as he arrived at the top of the steps.

"Welcome to the Temple of Baal!" the High Priest cried out to the crowd. "The giver of the winter rains, rider of the clouds, the Conqueror, the protector of our city. We have been commanded by our lord Baal to celebrate the first fruits of the land and of our flocks by bringing them as sacrifices to Baal's holy temple. I welcome all of you. Baal welcomes all of you."

Yoninah was impressed with the fine robes of the High Priest. Although she came yearly to this festival, its ceremony and rituals always impressed. The young people also appeared to be enmeshed in the ritual unfolding on the portico.

At this point, priests from inside the Temple carried on poles a palanquin on which stood a golden statue of a bull. Yoninah said, "That represents Baal the Conqueror, the god of strength and virility." The statue was splendidly worked with horns of ivory and eyes of onyx. The golden figure, almost life-sized, usually resided in the Holy of Holies and was brought out only for special occasions. The Feast of Baal was one such occasion. Music accompanied the pageantry of the statue's appearance. Ten priestesses in long white robes flanked the figure of the bull, as did musicians with lutes and lyres. The priestesses began to sing a prayer to Baal. Their ten voices, in unison, were strong and carried across the plaza.

Prayer to Baal

Arise, O Baal!

May your enemies be scattered.

And may your foes flee before you!

Sing to Baal, chant hymns to his name;

Extol him who rides the cloud;

The Lord is his name.

The High Priest repeated the first line of "Arise O Baal, may your enemies be scattered, may your foes flee before you" as the celebrants sang along, with their right arms raised in their heartfelt praise of Baal's strength.

"Now, let us go and celebrate the strength of Baal, the protector of our beloved city," the High Priest concluded. "Let the girls and women dance around the Asherah tree, in honor of El's consort, the great goddess Asherah. Then we will offer a fragrant offering to the gods. And finally, we shall all partake in this feast of celebration!"

Bat-El was enraptured by all the drama before her. She clearly marveled at the appearance of the High Priest, the statue of the Bull, at the spectacle of priestesses and musicians.

Laylah said, "This is wonderful!" Yoninah suspected that the incense burning throughout the plaza was contributing to her sense of wonder.

Laylah insisted on heading to the Asherah tree, with Bat-El in in hand, Yoninah and Tahir following close behind.

Laylah eagerly joined the circle of dancing girls, as they twirled around the great tree in the middle of the plaza. She pulled Bat-El into the circle.

Yoninah went to sit down on a bench nearby. Tahir stood watching the dancers. The barefoot young girls were dressed in finery, their long black hair flying every which way as they twirled.

Tahir continued to watch for a bit longer. He spoke with Yoninah: "Bat-El and Laylah seem safe enough." He eyed a group of young men who stood at a respectful distance from the dancing women. Tahir noticed that the men were drinking red wine. "I am going to get a cup of wine as well. Did you want one?" he asked Yoninah. She said, "Yes, just a small cup is enough for me." He went to a nearby cask and returned with two cups.

BatEl and Laylah danced for an hour. Then, the young men were finally allowed to join in the revelry. Yoninah kept a close eye on the situation. Tahir kept an even closer eye.

He said, "I do not trust these young men. They look like schemers and ruffians to me. I am going to pull the girls out of the circle. They would no doubt take advantage of a girl if given half a chance."

Yoninah suspected that Tahir was being overly protective, but she nodded her agreement nonetheless.

Laylah was holding hands with one of these young men, Tahir tapped her on the shoulder and pulled her out of the circle. The young man, maybe sixteen at the oldest, had a beard just beginning to grow in. Not a great threat, on the face of it. But Tahir had evidently decided that he looked like a lout anyway.

Yoninah could hear the conversation that ensued. "Why did you do that?" asked Laylah. "We were having fun!"

"Your mother said to keep an eye on you girls. And I do not trust that boy you were holding hands with," Tahir trailed off as Laylah's dance partner marched over.

"Who are you? Her brother or something?" the young man asked.

"I am her guard," Tahir said sternly. "Do you have a problem with that?"

Yoninah saw the young man taking note of Tahir's broad shoulders and the fierceness of his posture. He stepped back a few feet, muttering under his breath something inaudible. The youth quickly rejoined the circle.

Yoninah smiled at Tahir's presumption and at his evident jealousy. Laylah did not take it that easily. "You had no right to interfere. I am not going to talk to you again, so there!" Laylah stomped off with Bat-El trailing behind.

The two sisters sat on a bench adjoining the one that Yoninah sat on. They sat in sulky silence for a short time. Tahir sat nearby. By then it was time for the feast.

Yoninah told the young people: "People have come from the outlying towns, bringing their offerings to Baal. Those who tend sheep and goats have brought the first-born of their flocks. Those who tend fields have brought barley from their spring harvest."

She went on: "The priests received these offerings. They sacrificed the animals according to ritual. They put the choice cuts on the sacred altar for roasting, on the altar built into the terrace of the Tower. The odor of the sacrifice is rising to the heavens, to make a pleasant offering to the gods."

"Bat-El said, "I am hungry. Do we get to eat too?" Her mother pointed out circular clay ovens situated throughout the plaza, each oven burning firewood in its lower level. The flames were visible through the openings in the front of the ovens. Attendants were placing cuts of meat on bronze racks in the ovens. Pointing to a nearby oven, Yoninah said: "There is your dinner, dear. They are roasting the cuts of meat right now."

Soon, the aroma of roasted goat and lamb filled the plaza. Temple attendants told the celebrants to come take a serving of roasted meat and a piece of bread made from the barley harvest. The roasted meat made a rare treat, so it was truly a day for celebration.

The drums had been beating throughout. Yoninah noticed that the drummers had finally stopped. Perhaps they were eating as well, she thought. As evening stole over the plaza, torches were lit. The incense altars continued to burn myrrh and cannabis.

Tahir offered to get food for the group. They continued sitting on the benches that lined the plaza. Yoninah noticed that

Laylah had forgotten she was angry with Tahir. She took the food she was offered. She asked Tahir to get her a cup of wine as well.

"All right, one cup," he said. Bat-El wanted a cup as well. "You're only ten years old. You can have wine mixed with lots of water."

The flickering lights of the torches cast dancing shadows. Yoninah was getting tired. Wine had its effect, as did the heady smoke of the incense. By this point of the evening, the youngest at the celebration were also getting tired. Some of the youngsters were going home. Those who were closer to adulthood stayed and danced.

Yoninah saw some of the couples go off to the margins of the plaza, to a stand of trees, where they sought shadowed recesses for privacy.

She decided it was time to take the girls home. Tahir agreed. Laylah argued but not too much. It had been a long day. And Bat-El was half-asleep by then, anyway.

Chapter 16: VIVID DREAMS

Yoninah had always had vivid dreams. She often talked to her mother in these dreams. Her mother had been dead for the last year. In the dreams, they would be having a companionable cup of wine together.

"Aren't you dead?" Yoninah would ask in the dreams.

"No, that was a mistake. I am fine," Yoninah's mother would reply.

Yoninah would go on to have a conversation which usually involved her mother complaining about her relatives. Yoninah found these dreams comforting.

But last night, after she and the young people came back from the Baal Festival, her dreams had taken a darker turn.

As they went to bed, Menelaus had told her about a drunk sailor in the harbor bar. Some madman talking out of his mind about being kidnapped by pirates. Ranting and raving about being a prisoner on their ship for two months and having just escaped. He was going on and on about how these pirates would take a city in a lightening quick raid, kill its defenders, then pillage and ransack it.

As the pirates left, the drunken sailor swore they would set the city ablaze behind them. He kept talking about "the burning, the burning." Menelaus said he felt sorry for the poor fellow. The sailor clearly had had too much to drink.

As improbable as the story was, it still affected her dream life. When she fell asleep, she had a wild dream in which she was escaping from a burning city. She was with her daughters as they fled through the streets of Ugarit, trying to avoid burning arrows and embers from burning houses. The King's Guard was urging them to go faster and telling them in what direction to go. At some turns, the street was filled with flames, and they would flee down another street. The flight seemed endless.

Yoninah woke up, with a wild feeling of panic as her heart raced. She realized she was back in her own bedroom. The household idols were sitting on the table opposite the bed. Baal looked protective, El looked kindly, and Asherah looked maternal as always. Yoninah saw the morning light streaming in from the slit of a window. She saw Menelaus sleeping peacefully beside her. She took a deep breath to calm herself down.

Yoninah knew the dream was a response to the wild story told by a drunk sailor. She felt foolish for letting it affect her. She vowed not to mention it to Menelaus. She didn't want to reveal herself as overly sensitive and easily frightened.

What a foolish dream, Yoninah thought to herself as she got out of bed. She gratefully picked up the pieces of her ordinary life in her little house on the southern margin of Palace Street. She savored the daily challenges of feeding a family and of tending to her shop. She was grateful for the small arguments between sisters and the push and pull of wills in raising children. Yoninah hoped she never had that dream again.

PART 2: STORM CLOUDS GATHER IN THE CITY

The king had seen, in a dream-vision, that the city would be destroyed. The palace would be shaken, its treasures dispersed. Of his dream vision, he let only his heart know. He put it not on his tongue, spoke of it with no man.

The roaring storm, which no one could oppose…enemy soldiers were coming to their gates.

--Adopted from "Curse of Akkad" a city destroyed ca. 2000 BC. See Coogan, 2013.

CHAPTER 17: A BANQUET, A MESSENGER

Midsummer had arrived. The days were long. The harbor was crowded with ships from all over the Great Sea.

The King held another banquet in the Palace. This banquet was in honor of the envoy from Nippur, from the heart of the Tigris-Euphrates River valley. The King and his court wanted to remain on friendly terms with the mighty Babylonian empire to the east.

Also in attendance was Hadid, an envoy from Tyre. At six days' sail further south along the coast, Tyre was a major seaport. Perhaps not as grand as Ugarit, but close.

The dinner was held in the Great Hall with King Ammurabi joined by both of his wives, as well as Thut-Moses and Urtenu. The latter, as the master of trade in Ugarit, was obliged to make small talk with his fellow merchants from Nippur and Tyre.

The Great Hall looked splendid. Alabaster vases were scattered throughout, filled with brightly colored flowers from the palace gardens. Light from the setting sun streamed into the room, courtesy of the open doors to the veranda. A light breeze blew swept through the gathering as well.

Guests were seated on fine chairs with comfortable goatskin throws and footstools. Serving girls provided small tables placed next to each guest's chair. Other servants brought plates of roasted lamb, seasoned with cumin and pepper from the lands of Arabia. Also on the table were the fresh fruits of the season such as figs, dates and pomegranates, as well as fresh bread and the finest olive oil for dipping.

The King sat at one side of the circle of chairs and low tables, flanked by his two wives, with Urtenu nearby. Taking a chair near the King and Urtenu, the envoy from Nippur entertained them with stories of the donkey caravans that traveled from the heart of Babylonia. The caravans followed the great highway along the banks of the Euphrates River. Stopping at the city of Mari, the caravans would then take the road towards the west, to the city of Ugarit. Or heading south, to the city of Tyre. An excellent Tant route, the envoy from Nippur assured them, because it skirted the desert to the south.

Hadid, the envoy from Tyre, took a seat next to Thut-Moses. The two of them got into a lively conversation. Hadid was handsome, in his middle years. He looked distinguished with a neatly trimmed beard and thick hair that was an admixture of black and gray. They talked about trade routes, the problems with pirates in the Aegean Sea; about letters flying back and forth from one king to another, to arrange trades or to ask for favors. Hadid complimented Thut-Moses on his extensive knowledge of languages. He said, "If ever the King is willing to let you go, you should come to Tyre. We can use a man of your skills." Thut-Moses said, "I am flattered." And that was the end of that conversation.

The evening took a wild swerve to a different topic sometime later. Although Thut-Moses did store away the emissary's offer for further consideration.

****

After dinner, wine was served as well as honey cakes and dates. David the king's musician appeared. He carried with him a fine-looking lyre. Torches were lit in the great hall, as the evening grew late.

"Our bard will tell us the story about a young hero named Aquat," the King said.

"This is an old story, repeated for generations here in Ugarit. We hope you enjoy it."

Tale of Aquat

David chanted, with a rhythm augmented by notes of the lyre:

Danel was a good man: a judge, a righteous man

The gods favored him. But he had no son.

He went to the Temple and prayed to the gods.

For seven days and nights, he prayed for a son.

Baal heard his prayer.

He asked his father El to bless Danel, saying:

'Let him have a son in his house,

An heir inside his palace...

To send his incense up from the earth

The song of his burial place from the dust.

To shut the jaws of his oppressors

To drive off his oppressors.

To hold his hand when he gets drunk.'

David sang this rousing verse a second time. The verse had a lively rhythm when accompanied by the lyre. Everyone could appreciate the value of a son. Especially the line about "holding his hand when he gets drunk." The guests raised a cup of wine when they got to that part. David continued the tale:

The gods granted Danel's prayer.

His wife conceived and the child was born.

They named the boy "Aquat."

He grew up into a handsome young man.

One day, Kothar-wa-Hasis, craftsman of the gods…

He came to visit the house of Danel.

He brought a present: a bow and arrows of his own making.

Danel gave the magical bow and quiver to his beloved son.

Now David played a run of notes that were discordant and ominous. He went on with his recitation.

Now Anat was the daughter of El.

A fierce warrior-goddess, quick to anger.

She saw the bow and arrows and wanted them for herself.

She approached Aquat and said to him:

'Listen, Aquat the Hero.

Ask for silver, and I'll give it to you.

For gold – I'll make it yours.

But give your bow to Anat,

let the Mistress of the Peoples have your arrows.'

Hadid whispered to Thut-Moses: "Oh no, Anat is not to be trifled with! She is going to kill the boy. We have this story in Tyre." The bard continued the story.

The boy refused to give her the bow and arrows.

Anat said: ' Give me the bow.

And I will give you eternal life.

Immortality-I will make it yours.'

Aquat replied : 'Immortality is only for the gods.

There is no such thing for ordinary men.

And I have something to else to tell you:

Bows are for warriors – do women ever hunt?'

Hadid again whispered to Thut-Moses. "A nice little speech. About immortality. Maybe he should have omitted the comment about women warriors, though."

Thut-Moses laughed. He was beginning to enjoy Hadid's running commentary. Queen Donitaya, sitting with the King at the far end of the circle of chairs and tables, looked at him when she heard the laugh. She smiled. She could guess the context. She too had expressed strong opinions about Anat.

David again played a harsh series of chords and went on:

Anat was angry and sent a Warrior.

To kill the boy and take the bow and arrows.

She transformed the Warrior into a vulture.

The vulture found Aquat in the wilderness.

He struck the boy and killed him.

When he tried to fly back to present the prize to Anat…

He dropped it by accident in the ocean, and it was lost.

The storytelling continued, with one last episode:

Danel and his family mourned Aquat's death.

His sister, Pughat, discovered where the assassin lived.

Pughat dressed up – with kohl, rouge, and fine robes

and went to visit him at his house.

Hiding a dagger underneath her robes.

He thought she was his consort.

She gave him cups of wine to drink and got him drunk.

And she killed him when he passed out.

"Well done!" whispered Hadid. "A fitting revenge."

Queen Donitaya asked for more wine for herself and for the room. She announced in a loud voice to the guests: "Stories about Anat always make me want to drink more wine."

****

Before the guests finished their last cup of wine and got ready to go home, a courier arrived. The man looked dusty and muddy. He had evidently traveled a long distance without stopping.

"I am from Carchemesh, from Hittite lands," the messengers said formally. "King Suppiluliuna sends this letter to King Ammurabi.."

The messenger handed a clay tablet to the King, who scanned it briefly and handed it to Thut-Moses. The room fell quiet as the guests turned their attention to the rare event of a message so important that it intruded on a royal occasion.

Thut-Moses scanned the tablet quickly.

"It is a matter of some sensitivity," Thut-Moses said softly to the King. "Do you want to discuss this in private?"

"Too late," the King raises his cup of wine. "Its arrival is now public knowledge. Go ahead and read it out loud."

Thut-Moses stood next to the King and translated the Hittite script.

"There are enemy soldiers at our borders," Thut-Moses read to the entire room. "With shields and lances and barbarian helmets. Send reinforcements. Send your army!'

"It is signed by King Suppiluliuma, with his seal, your highness," said Thut-Moses.

Silence greeted this pronouncement.

"This is grave news," the King said. "We will go ahead and ask our guests to go home. And then decide how to respond."

The dinner guests looked stricken at this decision. But they took the King at his word and bundled up in their cloaks and headed towards the great doors of the dining hall. Hadid gave a solicitous touch to Thut-Moses' arm, and said, "I hope to see you in Tyre someday," and he made his exit. The envoy from Nippur also left quickly. "No doubt planning expeditious returns to their separate homelands," thought Thut-Moses.

The King told his two wives to go ahead and kiss the children good night. Queen Donitaya, whose facial expressions Thut-Moses could read easily after their sessions together, looked afraid. As well she should, thought Thut-Moses. The Queen was a smart woman. The message meant the almighty Hittite army could no longer defend the empire of Ugarit.

In contrast, the second Queen looked untroubled as she left the banquet. She usually left affairs of state to her husband.

After the guests had made their precipitous departure, the King turned to Thut-Moses and Urtenu.

"This the first time I have heard of a land force penetrating into Hittite territory." The King asked that his Chief Advisor be summoned, the one with spies everywhere, to ask what he knew of these foreign fighters.

Even though the hour was growing late, Thut-Moses sent a messenger to bring the Chief Advisor to the great hall.

The Chief Advisor appeared a few minutes later. He was a small man, with a narrow face and eyes that were too close together. Thut-Moses always thought he looked like a weasel. The King meanwhile referred to him as his "Eye" – a nickname for "spy".

Thut-Moses again read the missive out loud.

"Can you make any sense of this matter?" the King asked the Chief Advisor.

The Chief Advisor was usually quite voluble, with an excess of flowery speech. This time, he spoke reluctantly.

"There have been rumors of large numbers of people migrating from the north," the advisor said. "There have also been rumors of the Kaska and other tribes on the flanks of the Hittite empire on the march. I thought these rumors were unfounded and did not mention them before to your majesty."

The King cleared his throat at the news.

"These unnamed foreign tribes, from what the Hittite king's message says, they appear to be nibbling at the margins of the Hittite Empire," the advisor continued.

This pronouncement was followed by a protracted silence in the great hall. The words of the Chief Advisor echoed against the stone walls of the room.

The eunuch gently broke the silence.

"It is growing late, my king," Thut-Moses said. "Perhaps ask the General, General Boaz, to come first thing in the morning, to discuss this situation?"

"Yes, first thing in the morning, we can call a meeting of the Council," the King agreed. "Make it so, Thut-Moses."

The King turned to the messenger, who had stood silently during the exchange. "We will have an answer for you by mid-morning," the King said. "Come back in the morning."

Urtenu and the Chief Advisor also said they would return in the morning. That left King Ammurabi and Thut-Moses alone in the great hall.

"Send a messenger to the General's house, to meet in the morning," the King said. "Then come sit with me for a few minutes. One more glass of red wine. This will be a difficult night, to get any sleep."

The two of them shared a glass of wine before going to bed. It was better to have company in a storm, thought Thut-Moses. And it felt like a storm was brewing.

CHAPTER 18: THUT-MOSES
VISITS THE HEALER

The next morning, Thut-Moses woke up at first light. He had had a rough night, with bad dreams. Apparently, drinking red wine before bed did not suit him. Neither did a request from the Hittites for their army. He woke up with a searing headache.

He called for his attendant, to send word to General Boaz to meet later that morning, when the sun was halfway to its apex. That gave him some time to seek a remedy for his headache.

He would ordinarily have appealed to the court physician, but the situation was delicate. He did not want to share his distress with a court functionary. He decided to seek out a healer from the lower city. He had heard of one, a short distance down Palace Street.

In the time he had available before the scheduled meeting, he walked down to the healer's shop and knocked on the door decorated with the sign of the snake.

Yoninah answered the door promptly.

Yoninah looked over her visitor carefully. The man before her looked better-dressed, considerably taller and certainly darker than her other visitors.

"Yes, can I help you?" Yoninah said politely.

"I am seeking something to help with headaches," Thut-Moses said plainly. "And with sleeping. I have a headache right now and need to make it go away. And I slept poorly last night. Can I come in?"

Yoninah motioned him in, gesturing to a seat on a shadowed bench in her front room. Yoninah knew people with headaches often prefer to sit in the shadows, away from the light pouring in from the narrow window.

Yoninah noticed his gait appeared normal. She didn't see any obvious dizziness or injuries that could cause a headache. Thut-Moses squeezed his long legs beneath the bench with difficulty. Yoninah felt sorry for her patient, who was clearly in pain.

Yoninah said softly. "Some tea perhaps? With a potion added to help with pain?".

Yoninah called for her older daughter, Laylah. "Please prepare some hot water in a cup. We will brew some pain medicine for our guest. Perhaps a mixture of poppy seed extract and willow bark."

Laylah peered around the corner at the tall man hunched over in pain. Her mother added one more instruction.

"Add some honey to it, to make it palatable," Yoninah said. "Otherwise, it is too bitter to drink."

Yoninah walked to her shelves of herbals. She picked out the poppy seed extract and willow bark elixir and handed them to her daughter.

While her daughter was in the kitchen preparing the tea, Yoninah talked gently to her new client.

"Have you had these headaches before?"

"No, not often," Thut-Moses said. "Matters have come up, some issues at the Palace. They are weighty matters. My sleep last night was troubled, and I work up with this headache."

"You are from the palace?" Yoninah asked. "I knew you were not from the lower city. I have never seen you in these streets. What brings you out of the sacred halls of the palace? Is not your Egyptian physician skilled in these matters?"

Thut-Moses looked uncomfortable. "I did not want to worry the man," he said. "I did not want to discuss the situation with him. Not yet at least."

"You did not want him to know you have a headache?" asked Yoninah.

"Please, just give me something to take the headache away," Thut-Moses shut his eyes in pain.

"Are you the King's eunuch?" said Yoninah. "I have heard of you. My friend met you some time ago in the tavern. He said you looked like the king's eunuch, but you said you were just an envoy from Egypt." She smiled gently at him.

"Yes, I am indeed in the service of the King," Thut-Moses said. "And it is of utmost importance that any concerns from the palace not become a source of gossip in the streets. So please, do not tell anyone of my visit."

"I can tell my daughter to say nothing," Yoninah said. "She will be back in a few minutes with some tea for you to drink. It is strong enough to take away a headache but not so strong it will make you fall asleep. Will that suffice?"

"That would be good," said Thut-Moses. He gave a half-smile to the healer. She found his face wonderfully expressive, even with a half-smile.

In a few minutes, Laylah came back with a cup of medicated tea. Thut-Moses drank the tea slowly.

"Sit a few more minutes, to make sure it suits you," Yoninah said.

Thut-Moses could feel the edges of the headache receding within a short time. He started looking around the healer's shop. He commented on the shelves of medicinal herbs, the mortar and pestle on the table, and the statues of Asherah in the alcove nearby.

"You have a fine figure of Asherah there," Thut-Moses said in a more conversational tone. "Is that a shrine to the goddess?"

The figure of Asherah stood on a pedestal. The goddess was done in bronze with an overlay of gold. She stood half a cubit tall, as a stately female figure with breasts and long hair and the insignia of her gender. Asherah looked kindly down on the healer's shop.

"Yes, that is my shrine," Yoninah said. "I ask the goddess for skill in healing. It can be a challenge, at times. I often offer a libation to Asherah. Perhaps you would like me to do that for you?

Thut-Moses nodded. As a terra-cotta figure, the goddess had a presence in every house in Ugarit. He knew she was the protector of the family.

"I am from Nubia, as you may have guessed," Thut-Moses said. "I trained in Egypt. In either country, we worship the goddess. We call her Isis but she is the same as Asherah. Just the name is different."

His color was improving. Although it was hard to say how she knew that, given that he was dusky to start with. His eyes were brighter, less shielded from the light. She thought his headache was getting better.

She stood up and walked to the pedestal with the goddess on it. There was a fine bronze bowl nearby.

Yoninah poured some wine into the bowl. "Goddess, who gives skill to the healer and gives healing to the sick, please ease this man's pain. Let him go back to the palace; to help the king and the court heal whatever distress has come upon them."

"An excellent blessing," Thut-Moses bowed his head.

"Here is some more medicine." She prepared two small bags for him. "Put a spoonful of each into a cup of hot water and let it brew for a few minutes. Add honey if you choose.

You can use it twice a day if the headache comes back. Any more than that, you will be sleepy and of no use to the King or Ugarit."

"Thank you," Thut-Moses said as he stood up and prepared to leave. He hesitated as he reached the door and turned around.

"Do you have a figure of Isis?" he asked. "Maybe it would help to invoke my native goddess. Maybe she could provide some added protection if danger arises."

Yoninah rummaged on the shelves and found a solid bronze medallion of Isis. She handed it to him, to hang around his neck on a leather thong. He hid it neatly under the cloak and tunic he wore. The bronze medallion, a fine piece of workmanship, included an inscription in hieratic.

"May the goddess spread her wings over me and protect me." Thut-Moses read the inscription aloud.

"The headache is almost gone," Thut-Moses said. "Thank you."

As he stood, his head almost touched the ceiling. He gave her twelve shekels for her trouble and for the medallion. She smiled at his words and at his height.

"May the Goddess be with you." Yoninah waved from the doorway.

Thut-Moses returned to the palace with restored strength, to face whatever trials lay in front of him. Little did he know how effective the bronze medallion would be in protecting him from dangers to come..

****

Meanwhile, Yoninah muttered to herself as she watched Thut-Moses walk away.

"The gods help us, if the King's eunuch is having trouble sleeping and is getting headaches. Not a good sign."

CHAPTER 19: THE KING'S COUNCIL MEETS

Later that morning, The King's Council met. In attendance were the usual players: the King, Thut-Moses, the Chief Advisor, and Urtenu.

General Boaz, a burly man in his late forties, also attended the meeting. With an erect posture, neatly trimmed beard, and the military style tunic that bespoke his high rank, he made a formidable appearance.

No wonder David was afraid of him, Thut-Moses thought to himself, remembering the bard's tale of being imprisoned after an affair with the General's wife.

At the head of the table sat the King. The royal face looked tense, with more worry lines across his brow.

"I have called this meeting because we have a message from the Hittite king," the King said. "There are enemies attacking his borders. King Suppiluliuma describes a standing army. He wants us to send our army as reinforcements."

"This is highly irregular," interjected the General. "The Hittite army is known throughout the civilized world as the finest of soldiers, with their chariots, archers, and fierce discipline. This is the first I have heard of any weakness on their part."

Thut-Moses felt a knot in his stomach. The King looked pale.

"The Hittites are dealing with famine. They have been asking for grain from Egypt. That no doubt has weakened them, left them vulnerable," said Urtenu.

And the Eye added: "My spies have picked up rumors of large numbers of people migrating from the north and possibly tribes on the border of the Hittites making a move on the Hittite's margins.

A pulse of silence filled the council chamber.

General Boaz was clearly unhappy to hear as much. "This is unfortunate. We are of course vassals to the Hittites and obligated by covenant to honor any request by Suppiluliama for military support. I never thought it would come to this."

"If we must send troops, it would take ten days to march them from Ugarit to Khatte, to Hittite territory," General Boaz mused. "A caravan of donkeys would be needed to carry supplies, along with scores of oxen-drawn carts. We can do it if necessary."

Another uncomfortable pause.

"That would leave the city walls unprotected, save for the King's Guard," the General added. "And the city walls need repairs. They are not as strong as they should be. The earthquake some years ago damaged them and they have not been fully patched. I would do this reluctantly, only if there is no other option."

"We will offer to send gold first," King Ammurabi said. "With gold, they can buy soldiers and weapons. We can send the letter today. The response would take at least five days."

Thut-Moses thought to himself that the King is trying to buy us more time.

"Do any of you have anything to add?" asked the King. The table was silent. And the messenger was dispatched back to the Hittites with an offer of enough gold to buy a hundred mercenaries.

****

Six days later, the King, Thut-Moses, General Boaz and the Chief Advisor met again. The offer of gold was declined. The Hittites needed the Ugarit army.

With a heavy heart, and further furrowing of his brows, the King ordered the mobilization of the troops. This could hardly be done secretly. Sending five hundred men as reinforcements for the Hittites from a city of eight thousand people would be noticed by everyone in Ugarit.

****

In the Palace, it felt like they were in the eye of a storm, with danger lurking just beyond the horizon.

Thut-Moses tried to tamp down his fears. He was busy catering to the King, reassuring him that the troops would return speedily. His words sounded hollow even to himself. How could he make a promise like that?

The King was drinking more red wine with honey, spending more time under the influence of cannabis and listening to the music of David. He kept talking about the colors of the notes.

Apparently, the King could see cascades of gold, red, green, and blue. He offered to share his cannabis-infused wine with Thut-Moses, but the eunuch declined. He figured one of them had to stay alert and functional.

In conversation with Queen Donitaya, Thut-Moses discussed the general sense of uncertainty in the Palace. The two of them, when not reading Ugaritic stories about King Kirte and the Baal epics, usually talked about the children's health or the heat of the day. This time, she mentioned that she was having bad dreams where she and her children were in danger—dreams that included swordplay, monsters, and fire, always fire. She said she would wake up quickly from these dreams.

"The dreams are upsetting. I am thinking of leaving the city, to go to our summer retreat. It is getting into the heat of summer." Queen Donitaya confided.

"Perhaps the danger will pass," Thut-Moses tried to sound reassuring, but it fell flat, even to his own ears. "Perhaps the troops will return."

"Perhaps," she said. "I am nonetheless going to start packing."

Thut-Moses had no response to this. He always thought Queen Donitaya was a smart woman. He valued her intuitions and her intellect. He too was having bad dreams.

****

The Queen and her attendants left a few days later. Donitaya had cajoled the second wife to join them. David's wife, who was beginning to show a pregnancy belly, joined them as well. The King had asked David to stay behind. Wagons loaded with their personal supplies, accompanied by guards, with donkeys and litters for the women and children, they headed towards their summer retreat. It would take two days to reach their destination: a heavily fortified royal compound, in a valley with access to fields and to pasturage for animals.

Thut-Moses and the Queen had spoken before her departure. "And you, my friend?" the Queen had asked. "What are you going to do if the city is attacked?"

"I will stay and fight with the King's Guards," Thut-Moses had said. "If we are overtaken, I will put down my weapons and surrender. I understand these marauders take captives. With luck, they will sell me to a ship heading for a haven further south. Where I can resume working as a scribe in a king's court."

The Queen had looked at him askance. "You are an interesting fellow," she had said. "An ambition to be taken captive? Me, I would rather languish in exile."

CHAPTER 20: UNEASE IN THE CITY

After the Army Departs

Under the blazing heat of summer, the city was growing uneasy. At the healer's shop, Yoninah started seeing more people complaining of bad dreams and trouble sleeping.

It was two weeks since the army had been mobilized. Five hundred men marching north, towards Hittite land, accompanied by a hundred donkeys laden with supplies and a caravan of oxen-carts as well. The citizens of Ugarit were aware of their leaving.

Most of the visitors to the healer were women worried about husbands or sons who had left with the army. The women invariably wanted a talisman, to the ask the favor of the gods to bring loved ones safely back. And a sleeping draught.

Among the visitors to the shop were Milchah and her daughter Sarai. The child was one of Yoninah's favorite patients. She had first met her as a three-year-old. She had watched her grow up into a delightful, bright six-year-old.

Milchah said, "My husband left with the army. I do not know when he will be returning.."

"My brother – his name is Yusef--he has come to Ugarit, to come get me and the children….to bring us to his house. It is five days away, in the mountains. We will stay with him until my husband comes back. I do not know how quickly we can return. It may be weeks; it may be months. Perhaps you can give us extra medicine? Sarai is doing well on her nightly teas. Her fits are less frequent and do not last as long…."

****

Yoninah remembered when she first met this family. The father had appeared at her door, early one morning. "Come quickly, my daughter is possessed by a demon. She is thrashing around and foaming at the mouth!"

The family's house was nearby. She had seen other patients said to be possessed by demons. She quickly gathered up the amulets and medicines she would need and went with him.

When she got to the family's home, she saw a small child on a bed. The child's arms and legs were shaking; her eyes were rolled back into her head. She was indeed foaming at the mouth. It had been a frightening sight.

A frenzied mother was standing next to the bed. She asked, "Will she be all right? Can you drive out the evil spirit?"

The mother told her that this fit had started only a short while before. This was her third such spell. She had fallen asleep after the other two spells and did not remember anything about them.

"She is a good girl. Why do these fits come on? She has done nothing to anger the gods. I do not understand."

Meanwhile, Yoninah took out her amulets and a small terra-cotta figure of Asherah. She put the clay figure on a table nearby. Then Yoninah started chanting an incantation to drive out demons. It was from the Mesopotamians, translated into Ugaritic. Her mother had taught it to her. She recited the incantation in a loud, firm voice:

"Whether you are a ghost that has come from the earth, or an evil demon… From this house you shall leave. From this chamber you shall leave!"

Yoninah then threw a clay figure of a demon to the ground. It smashed into a satisfying display of dismembered parts. It had an ugly face, with sharp teeth and a pig-like countenance.

It deserved to get smashed. The child's tremors had slowed down and finally ceased. She had closed her eyes and appeared to be asleep.

"I am going to give you some valerian root, to mix up in hot water as a tea," Yoninah said to the anxious mother. "Let her drink it, once she wakes up. She will need to take the medicine every night, before she goes to sleep."

She added, "I can teach you the incantation. I can give you extra figures of the demon to be smashed. Keep the figure of Asherah. She is the protector of children. Besides the incantations, the medicine will also help keep the demons away,"

"She should be all right. I see sweet children like this who get fits. She has done nothing wrong. We never know what makes the gods send a burden on one person and not another. Or why demons seek out one person and not another. But the incantations and the medicine should help."

Yoninah promised to return the next day, to see how the child she was doing and to give the mother more medicine. Yoninah's mother had taught her the usefulness of valerian root, not only as a sleep draught but also for the "falling sickness," as the Babylonians called it.

****

Six-year-old Sarai and her mother in her front room...going into the mountains for a stay of uncertain length. Yoninah of course gave Milchah extra valerian root. She prepared a leather bag with enough root to last a good six months.

The mother was grateful. She gave Yoninah some wool for her help and for the medicine. Enough wool to weave another cloak, thought Yoninah. Very generous. And helpful. Especially if she and her family were also going to be refugees from Ugarit and would need shelter and clothing on the road. She would give the wool to Gedalyah's grandmother, their neighbor next door. The grandmother was adept at weaving and would render it into a warm cloak. She would pay her in shekels for her trouble..

Yoninah was keenly aware of the danger the city faced. The army largely gone; the city walls unprotected. She was not overly superstitious. So far, largely undisturbed by bad omens or dreams. But the fact of the city's military vulnerability was hard to argue with.

Milchah wished her goodbye and gave her a hug. Sarai gave her a hug. Yoninah held the hug a little longer for the child. She would miss them, for however long they were gone.

CHAPTER 21: ANOTHER MESSENGER COMES TO COURT

Meanwhile, at the palace, despite the fact of the army having left two weeks before, everyone tried to pretend that things were normal. The effort at pretense was admirable, although it took a toll on all concerned.

On another day of scorching heat, with the stones of the courtyard blazing in the sun, another courier arrived at the palace gates. Escorted into the cool of the palace and into the grand hall, he brought another cuneiform tablet from the king of the Hittites and handed it ceremoniously to King Ammurabi.

Quickly summoned to the great hall, Thut-Moses scanned the tablet.

"Did our soldiers arrive in Hittite lands?" the King asked. "What does the message say?"

"No, no word of our soldiers," answered the scribe. He relived the scene from three weeks prior, when the first letter from the Hittite king had arrived. Hadn't they just done this?

Thut-Moses gathered his strength and translated the missive.

> *"Enemy ships are attacking our Aegean ports. They carry the black flag of pirates. They are ravaging our seaports, taking gold and captives as slaves. Then they set the cities to the torch. We need to cut off their access. Send your navy to Lukka, so we can establish a blockade."*

The King suddenly looked gaunt and ten years older. Clearly, this new message was a blow.

"Can you read it again?" the King asked.

Thut-Moses tried to keep his voice steady as he read it a second time. The second reading did not help. The creases across the king's forehead only deepened.

The King appeared to be at a loss. He stared off into the distance blankly.

"Another meeting of the council, my lord?" Thut-Moses suggested.

"Yes. Can you organize it? For as quickly as possible?" asked the King.

"With the admiral of the navy?" Thut-Moses asked.

The King nodded. Thut-Moses sent runners to the appropriate houses, to gather up the admiral as well as the usual players. The dusty, muddy messenger from the Hittites stood at attention until the King dismissed him.

"Rest for a bit," the King said. "We should have an answer for you within the day."

An hour later, for the second time in three weeks, the council met in the Palace, with Admiral Ahab in attendance this time. General Boaz had accompanied his troops to Hittite lands.

Admiral Ahab was a good-sized man, in his late fifties, with the deeply tanned skin of the lifelong sailor. He was a man of few words. Thut-Moses knew him in passing and always thought he parsed his words carefully.

The King asked Thut-Moses to read the letter to the council. A moment of dead silence followed his reading.

"Have any of you heard of enemy ships in the Aegean Sea? Or, for that matter, in the Great Sea?" the King asked.

The King looked straight at the Chief Advisor and repeated the question. "Have you heard of foreign ships?"

"My spies have told me of seagoing people moving in from the west in the Great Sea and from the countries to the north, from the Black Sea." The chief advisor's voice shook as he answered.

A chief advisor looking nervous was never good, thought Thut-Moses. He was beginning to think that the man would rather die than tell the King something unpleasant.

"I am told that these people have ships that can move swiftly, with oarsmen and sails." The Chief Advisor cleared his throat. "I have also gotten reports of piracy in the Aegean. Pirates have been pestering the Mycenean mainland and its islands."

Thut-Moses suddenly saw in his head a vision of enemies abroad in the seas just six days' sailing from Ugarit.

The King turned to Urtenu, the chief merchant. "Have you had any inkling of this?" the King demanded. "Has there been any word among the ships' captains of enemy ships in our waters?"

Urtenu fumbled a bit in answering. "My lord, there was one ship that went missing a bit over two months ago," Urtenu said. "We do not know if it was wrecked or was captured by pirates. Traffic in the harbor is lighter than it should be, especially ships expected from the Aegean."

"Admiral Ahab," said the King. "What do you think? My father, whom you served, did he ever have to deal with a situation like this?"

"No, my lord. This is unheard of," replied the Admiral. "We have always held onto our fleet, to protect our own waters. Except perhaps, for that one time, when we sent a few boats to Cyprus. I do not know whose ships these are, marauding in the waters along the Aegean. There are always pirates active in the Aegean. They are usually Myceneans whose numbers do not constitute a major threat. This sounds like new players, some group other than the local."

The room filled with silence as the council considered this information.

"What ships do we have, to send to Lukka?" Thut-Moses asked. "To the Aegean?"

"We have 100 ships we can send," replied the Admiral. "But that would leave our harbor largely unprotected from any seaward attack. I can organize the captains and get the crews called up and on board the boats within a day. Tell me what to do, my lord."

The King glanced at Thut-Moses. The King had come to rely more and more on the advice of his scribe. Thut-Moses nodded ever so slightly.

"Yes. Activate the fleet. Make it so." The King looked gutted. His face was pale and his hands trembled. This was a major blow to the city. Ugarit was a city of trade. Not a fortress, not a military super-power. He hoped the threat from the Aegean was short-lived and that he would see his ships again.

****

The ships left two days later. The fleet sailed away from White Harbor in the bright sun of a late summer day. Sailing northward, the Ugaritic oarsmen deftly navigating, their sails finally catching the wind. That morning, Thut-Moses was at the western side of the Palace. He had a good view of the harbor. He watched the fleet sail away. They became black dots on the horizon and then disappeared. He felt a weight in his chest.

That evening, Thut-Moses was dispatched to the King's chambers. The King asked him to sit with him. They drank a goblet of wine together. The King called for his musician, for David with the lovely voice. He listened to the notes of the lyre. Thut-Moses left the King to his music. He knew that his majesty found it helpful when he had trouble sleeping. Thut-Moses could also feel the effects of the wine. Thut-Moses welcomed the respite into sleep when it finally came.

****

"Summer, the time of death." That was a saying in the city. The time of death when Mot, the god of the underworld, reigns supreme. When the rivers dry and the crops burn in the sun. Many families of the upper classes flee to their summer homes. Those who live in the lower city, without the luxury of a retreat to the cooler climate of the mountains, seek shelter from the midafternoon heat in their home. The thick stone walls will protect them from the burning sun, but not from the impending attack.

CHAPTER 22: FURTHER UNEASE IN THE CITY

In Response to Sailing of the Ships

The afternoon heat baked the city streets. It was making people cranky. They had other reasons to be unhappy as well.

The people in the city had seen the troops march north, to Hittite land, three weeks before. They had watched the fleet of 100 ships sail out of the harbor the week before. Rumors were flying fast and furious throughout the city.

At the healer's shop, Yoninah saw yet more people complaining of bad dreams and anxiety. There had been a thousand men on board the ships that had left the harbor. This in addition to the hundreds of men who had left with the army.

One woman said, "I saw a gathering of twenty black crows in the city plaza. A brood of them like that…. It felt like a bad omen." She asked Yoninah, "Do you know what to expect? What does it mean if the crows gather?"

Yoninah said, "I do not know." But she felt a twinge of fear herself. She was usually immune to talk of evil omens. Less so at this point, in midsummer with the city walls undefended. The King's Guard had taken up posts at the watchtowers. But they were thin on the ground, only fifty of them.

Yoninah continued to make her weekly trips to the Temple quarters, to buy her medicines. This week, she waited until late afternoon for the heat to abate. As she traversed the length of Palace Street, she noticed that the street was quieter than usual. The crowd of sailors and scurrying slave girls had thinned.

Yoninah had heard of bands of self-anointed prophets in the hills outside the city, wandering around in a mist of a mind-altering hypnotic, playing instruments—lyre and drums-- and predicting the end of the world. She did not see the gray-haired, unkempt prophet from the spring, the one talking about a great wind, an earthquake, a fire, and then the voice of Baal. She wondered what became of him.

She bought a few execration pots from the shop selling them. They were almost sold out of "Let the foreigners flounder and sink!" She bought a figure of Asherah from the shop that sold terra cotta figures. They too were almost depleted in their stock. She also bought a few amulets, with blessings on them and invocations against demons.

The monkey man was no longer at his corner, she noticed.

She climbed up Palace Street and approached the finer houses near the Temple and the Palace. Many of the houses were boarded up. The families of the elite had packed up and left for their summer retreats. Yoninah thought, "They have quietly stolen away from the city."

As she reached the high point of the city and approached the Temple compound, Yoninah could see a plume of smoke rising from the terrace just below the tower. The priests were offering an enhanced schedule of sacrifices and prayers to Baal. The sacrificial fires were burning almost nonstop.

Just past the Temple Compound, she found her backstreet supplier. Yoninah was able to replenish her supplies of sleeping draughts, poppy extract, and cannabis. Although the price was higher than what she had paid for them the week before. The shopkeeper said, "The boats are not coming to the harbor. it's harder to get stock "And the sailors who do come, they tell me there are pirates and marauders swarming the Aegean Sea." Grateful that she had the herbals in hand, she said, "I hope things get better." The shopkeeper added, "Me, I have heard rumors of enemy ships approaching Ugarit. I am thinking of closing up shop for a week or two. Until this ill wind blows over."

This last statement threw her off balance. The man was no fool. If he was afraid enough to close the shop, she started thinking maybe it was time to leave the city.

She said, "May the gods protect us!" and bid him farewell.

As she made her way back home, she remembered the eclipse of the sun in early spring. How the bright sunlight disappeared, and dusk replaced it for a good hour. How the birds overhead became quiet. She decided that this had indeed been an omen sent by the gods. An omen of coming misfortune. She remembered the prophecy of destruction from the disheveled gray-haired man from an earlier excursion along Palace Street. She felt the cold stab of fear run through her.

CHAPTER 23: A LETTER FROM CYPRUS AND THE VISIT TO THE SEER

A week later, yet another courier arrived at the Palace. He brought a message from the king of Cyprus. Thut-Moses and the King were both on hand for its receipt. Thut-Moses translated:

"Enemy ships sighted off our west coast, twenty ships flying a foreign flag. Some of them look like they are from Ugarit. Have your own ships gone rogue against you and taken up piracy? Be aware of the danger."

The King said: "Foreign ships are in the Great Sea! The blockade at Lukka did not work. They somehow got past it, got beyond the Aegean and entered our waters!"

Thut-Moses was equally concerned. "Yes, your majesty. That seems to be the case…It is worrisome. We have gotten back no word from the ships we sent to Lukka. I hope they survived whatever engagement there was…."

The King called for his Eye, the Chief Advisor. "The man with the face of a weasel," thought Thut-Moses again. It was harder to trust a man with such a face.

He asked his Eye: "Have you heard any reports of foreign marauders in the Great Sea? Have any of our ships been overtaken by foreigners? And thus appearing in the fleet of twenty that Cyprus reports?"

His Eye said: "Reports of marauders? I have indeed just gotten reports, your Majesty, of attacks on seaports in Mycenaean territory. It is unclear if these are foreign attackers or one city-state fighting another. The reports are confusing, sire. There is too much uncertainty at this point." He continued: "As for your second question: 'Have any of our ships been commandeered by foreign pirates?' There are two ships that have gone missing. They could well have been hijacked by pirates. We have no formal reports as yet."

"How quickly can ships get from the western coast of Cyprus to our shores?" asked the King.

"If the winds were in their favor, my lord, it would take at least five days to get from the west coast of Cyprus to Ugarit.

If they were indeed heading this way, "answered the Councilor.

Thut-Moses said, "Four days to plan a response, my liege… if they are headed this way."

The King told the Eye: "I want daily reports for now. Let me know if you hear anything else. You are dismissed for today."

When they were left alone, The King began to pace. He said to Thut-Moses. "I am in a quandary. What response can we make to this news? We have no navy, no army. If a fleet of enemy ships appears in our harbor, what recourse do we have?"

****

Thut-Moses gave it some thought and replied, "We can ask Cyprus to send ships. We can ask Carchemesh to send troops."

"There may not be enough time," said the King. "We have a narrow margin. It will take some days for a ship to carry a letter to Cyprus and a response to return…A courtier to Carchemesh and back would take even longer. Probably a week. We may be out of time."

Thut-Moses said, "You may be right, my lord. If help does not arrive in the next few days, we need to plan an evacuation."

"Yes," the King said. "An evacuation. I am feeling like the gods have abandoned us. I need some words of comfort. Can we seek out a seer? An oracle. Perhaps it will be reassuring. I need reassurance."

The king went on, "The priest of Baal, the old one who died last year, he was supposed to be a prophet. He claimed to be able to channel the voice of the gods. Perhaps I could seek him out."

"But he's dead, my lord. You said as much," said Thut-Moses."

The King went on as if his aide had not spoken. "The seer in the lower city, she is supposed to be able to bring up a shade from the land of the dead and to talk to him," said the King. "Perhaps she can ask for guidance from the gods, on my behalf.,"

The King looked so woebegone that Thut-Moses decided not to argue with him. Perhaps the seer would bring him comfort of some kind.

"We can go, then, my lord, if you wish, to see this woman. When do you want to go?" asked the eunuch.

"Right now. Let us wear cloaks that hide our faces and seek her out right now!"

It was one of those rare days in summer when it was cloudy and spitting rain. With their faces hidden in their hooded cloaks, they were able to pass unnoticed along the length of Palace Street.

The seer's house was almost on the outskirts of town. They found her modest house and knocked on the door. A young man answered.

"Can I help you?" he said.

"We are looking for the old woman, the seer. Is she here? We want to talk to someone who died last year. She can raise the dead, can't she?" asked the King.

"She is here. She is my grandmother. Have a seat here, in the courtyard. I will go tell her what you said," answered the boy.

He was gone for several minutes. When he returned, he led them to a small, dark room "This feels like a cave," the king whispered to Thut-Moses. "I do not like caves." There was incense burning on altars throughout the room. They could identify the mixed aromas of cannabis, myrrh, and frankincense. It was a heady combination. There were small lamps lit in the corners of the room. A small slit of a window high up in one wall provided a scant amount of light and ventilation.

Amongst the vapors, they could see the seer. She was an elderly woman with wild gray hair.

"Welcome, my lords. What can I help you with?" she asked.

"I want to talk with Yahu-El, the old priest from the Temple. He died a year ago. Can you reach him?" said the King.

The vapors were growing thicker. The King said, "I feel strange." He took off his heavy cloak. And he started moving his hands, seemingly fascinated by their arcs as he swept them back and forth in front of him. The eunuch said, "It is the vapors, my liege." He too felt like his speech was slow; he could see colors and shapes form with each word he uttered.

"Very well, my lords, I shall summon the shade of Yahu-El for you," the woman said."

She approached a pit in the floor of the room that they had not noticed before. The pit was demarcated with a circle of bricks, each inscribed in cuneiform. The eunuch said, "Those inscriptions are invocations to Mot, the god of the underworld." They were both impressed and frightened.

The seer then started chanting. "O great lord Mot, keeper of the netherworld, keeper of the souls of those who have left us, we beseech you, send to us the soul of Yahu-El. He joined you no more than a year ago." She recited, in Ugarit, the same incantation ten times in a row. In a sing-song voice, as she swayed back and forth in a pose of prayer, her right hand lifted high.

A dark shadow appeared above the pit. Whether it was the shade of a man or not was hard to say. The lamps lit in this cave of a room gave a flickering light, no more. The king said: "Yahu-El, is that you?" And the seeress said, "He says yes." But the king and the eunuch could hear nothing. The witch-woman said, "I can hear him. Ask him what you want."

"The city is at risk," said the King. "There are enemy ships in the waters nearby. Will they attack and destroy us? Or will the ships we need, the army we need, will they come back in time to save us? Please, Yahu-El, we seek your counsel," said the King.

The vaporous shade continued to sway in the space above the pit. The witch said: "He says: "The city will burn.""

"No, let me ask him again!" cried the king. The shade had evaporated, dissipated into thin air.

The woman said: "He is gone, my liege. I am sorry. But those were his words, I am afraid: 'The city will burn.'"

The King was immobile at the edge of the pit. He was frozen in place, envisioning who knows what terrors. The eunuch gently took his arm and said, "We must go, my lord."

The eunuch gave a handful of silver shekels to the seer. Thut-Moses and the King took their cloaks and left. The King had been hoping for an oracle of salvation, not of doom. They made their way back, supposedly incognito, through the narrow streets of the city. Their heads cleared as they got further away from the incense and vapors in that confined space. Although people still looked at them askance. Perhaps their gait had not entirely returned to normal. They made it back safely to the Palace Gate.

****

After they leave, the old woman packed up her things, grabbed her grand-son, and fled the city. She decided to close the shop. And to join the refugees who had started to trickle out of the ill-omened city. "If the King needed to talk to a shade that badly, that is not a good sign," she said.

CHAPTER 24: AT THE PALACE: WORD OF ENEMY SHIPS

A week after their unsettling trip to the seer's house, Thut-Moses was feeling increasingly uneasy. Neither Cyprus nor Carchemesh had replied to the King's pleas for aid. The city of Ugarit was completely unprotected. Thut-Moses kept seeing the specter of enemy ships prowling in the nearby Great Sea.

Thut-Moses sat at his table in the comfort of his apartment. He tried to concentrate on reading a scroll but found himself too distracted. A palace guard appeared at his door, reporting that two men from the harbor had just arrived at the palace gate, claiming to have important news for the king. Did Thut-Moses want to see them?

"Of course, let them in," Thut-Moses said after a moment of hesitation.

When the two visitors were escorted into the room, Thut-Moses was surprised to recognize the Mycenean from the tavern, the one who had quickly penetrated his attempt at a disguise. The man who introduced himself as Menelaus. Thut-Moses had thought it was a rather weighty name at the time. Accompanying him was the same youth of stocky build and with surprisingly light-colored eyes, probably an Afghani from the caravans.

Menelaus gave a nod of recognition to the tall black man, now in courtly garb.

"What is this important news from the harbor?" Thut-Moses asked, rising to his feet to greet his visitors.

"We work at the harbor, my lord," the older man said. "We load and unload cargo for the ships that come into Ugarit. You are the king's scribe and aide if I remember. I am Menelaus and this is Tahir."

"Yes, I remember you." Thut-Moses took one look at their distraught faces. "Please sit down." Thut-Moses gestured to two benches nearby and offered them beer or wine, whichever would make the story unfold more quickly. They both chose wine, and Thut-Moses' attendant silently brought out three cups.

"Our harbor master sent us. We got word of enemy ships not far from Ugarit. Two cities were looted and burnt, one of them within half-day sail from Ugarit. He wants the King to know," said Menelaus.

Thut-Moses stared hard at Menelaus, prolonging the silence for a few beats. Then the eunuch regained his composure.

"It is already growing late in the day," Thut-Moses said this as calmly as he could manage. "Why such news so late in the day?"

Menelaus looked exhausted. Tahir took up the story.

Tahir answered the question posed by the scribe.

"I was there, watching as a ship came late into the harbor, my lord. The ships that come late in the day, they are usually seeking a berth for the night. Can't navigate in the dark, you know."

"Go on," said Thut-Moses.

"This ship, it was from Miletos. Heavy in the water, laden with goods. The captain, he was an Aegean fellow. He disembarked quickly, came down the gangplank and into the shallow water at top speed. He was shouting: 'Foreign ships! Half-day sail from here! Heading this way, no doubt!'"

"Now this fellow has berthed at White Harbor before. But this time, he said: 'Not seeking a berth tonight. We want to put on water, other supplies and head out again. While we still have some light. There's a cove down the way; we will shelter there for the night.'"

Menelaus took up the narrative at this point. "The shouting and hubbub drew my notice and that of the harbor master who came to see what all the noise was about, plus every other man at the harbor that day. The harbor master – he's a good man, been there for twenty years, knows his way around – wanted more information.

'What did you see? Where were these enemy ships?'

"The captain answered in a loud voice that carried across the crowd gathered to hear the story. He went on: 'We've been at sea now for seven days. The trip was smooth and uneventful until yesterday. We were heading into the harbor at Ibn-Geir – a little town, with a harbor well-sheltered from the waves – last night towards sunset. As we approached the town, we could make out foreign ships beached on their shore. Three of them. Lightweight ships, built for speed, with oars for eighteen. And another four ships just offshore, with the same build. The same birds' heads at the prow and stern. And strange looking men – in kilts, with odd helmets on their heads, loading up loot into their ships. The men carried fierce-looking swords and shields. And the city burning behind them. They had torched the city. It was getting dark. We could make out the flames.'"

Thut-Moses interrupted with a question. "This ship from Miletos, was it attacked?"

Menelaus went on, "No, my lord. They turned the ship around, rowed away with all their might, and took shelter a distance away. That's what their captain said."

"And then?" asked Thut-Moses. "They sailed to Ugarit?"

Menelaus took a sip of wine and turned to Tahir to continue the story.

"Aye, your honor. They did. The captain said they had a late start in the morning. Something about repairing a sail. By the time they got to Ben Endi, the next port along the sea, they could tell that the marauders had gotten there before them. Ben Endi was burning."

"Ben Endi is close," said Thut-Moses. "Too close for comfort."

"Yes, it is," said Menelaus. "If the sea raiders shelter somewhere for the night, they can be at Ugarit by morning."

"Did the harbor master shut down the harbor?" Thut-Moses asked Menelaus.

"He shut down the harbor as soon as he could. He makes quick decisions. He sent some men to fetch water and provisions for the Aegean ship. Then the harbor master sent others to secure the storehouse. Finally, he sent most of us home, to warn our families and to start packing in case they must flee the city in the morning. Nobody stayed to argue with him, either. The harbor master, he sent me and Tahir to the palace to get word to the king."

"There you have it," said Menelaus. "We had to let you know as fast as possible. Me and Tahir here, we walked at top speed through the streets." He took another sip of the sweet wine, likely to settle his nerves, thought Thut-Moses.

Thut-Moses asked his attendant to get him a cup of wine as well. He sipped at it slowly, as he digested the news that the Mycenean and his friend had brought. He put his elbows down on the table, closed his eyes, and rubbed his forehead. Seeing if that would make his brain work any faster.

When he opened his eyes again, Menelaus and the youth were still there. And the city's imminent danger still a reality. He had hoped it had been a hallucination. Apparently not.

The three of them sat in silence for several minutes. Then Menelaus cleared his throat.

"Should we stay, my lord, and share this directly with the king?"

"Yes, we can rest in my chambers for a bit longer," Thut-Moses said. "The King should be done with dinner soon. I will send my attendant to give him word. We can go meet him in the throne room."

Thut-Moses told his attendant to quickly go to the King's dinner.

"Tell him it is an emergency," Thut-Moses said to the attendant. "We need to talk with him. You can tell him that Enemy ships are nearby, but do not tell anyone else. Do you understand?"

The attendant, a middle-aged man, nodded gravely and left immediately to bring word to the King.

Shadows were growing long on the courtyard by then, as Thut-Moses, Menelaus and Tahir, crossed its expanse a few minutes later, heading to the royal quarters for an audience with the King.

"I want you two to tell the story just as you told me," Thut-Moses said. "Answer any questions he asks you. We should be able to send you back to your homes this night, with enough time left for you to start packing as well. I don't see any alternative because we need to empty the city of women and children."

"And dogs," mumbled Tahir. Thut-Moses looked at him quizzically, as they finished crossing the courtyard and gained the royal quarters.

****

As they entered the throne room. Thut-Moses saw Menelaus and his young companion scan its sumptuous furnishings. The eunuch looked pained as Menelaus approached the throne and made a clumsy bow. The older man was clearly not schooled in palace protocol.

"What is this about?" the King asked. "What is this talk of enemy ships?"

"We have been sent by the harbor master to tell your majesty that enemy ships have attacked and burnt two nearby towns." Menelaus cleared his throat.

"Go on," ordered the king.

"A crew arriving from the north said they had seen a fleet of seven foreign ships, unlike any seen in Ugaritic territory before: shallow draft, sleek ships with eighteen oars apiece and with warriors armed with cutting swords and leather shields. Their ships had strange bird heads at the prow."

"They reported having seen two towns burning along the coast. The first was Ibn -Geir, the second Bar Endi."

The king was stunned by this report. "Why, that is close by! And they are heading this way?"

"There is every reason to believe they are indeed headed to Ugarit. It would be ripe for the pickings, your majesty."

The king asked further questions and got answers he did not like. He and Thut-Moses discussed the situation in a conversation that grew heated. The King's face lost its color. His hands were shaking.

"That letter we sent to Cyprus, have we gotten any response yet? Are they sending ships or not?" the King demanded.

"No, my liege." Thut-Moses bowed his head. "We are expecting a response today. It has not arrived yet."

The king looked stricken at this reply. Thut-Moses thanked Menelaus and Tahir for their mission and told them to go back to the harbor or to their homes, as they thought best.

Thut-Moses then walked with them to the street. The eunuch gave them a bag of shekels for their efforts to warn the king.

"You might need some silver in the next few days." Thut-Moses said. "You two look fit and healthy. If we need to evacuate the city, we will need men like you to help defend the city walls, to give the citizenry time to flee. But you two, go home and get your families packed up. There will likely be an evacuation in the morning. The afternoon is growing late, and the streets will be dark soon. First light is the earliest we can manage."

****

As they reached the street in front of the palace, Thut-Moses noted that it was quieter than usual. "Fewer people are afoot than usual." Menelaus nodded his agreement. The once-bustling street was quiet...except for the flock of crows circling overhead.

CHAPTER 25: LAST DAY IN THE PALACE

After Menelaus and Tahir left, the response from Cyprus finally arrived in the Palace. This was in response from the King's requests for ships from Cyprus to help fend off what looked like an imminent attack.

The King of Cyprus offered the following advice:

If you have indeed spotted enemy ships at sea, make yourself as strong as possible. Now, where are your own troops and chariotry stationed? Are they not stationed with you? If not, who will deliver you from the enemy forces? Surround your town with walls; bring troops and chariotry inside. Then wait in full strength for the enemy.

The King and Thut-Moses were both angry. Their situation looked even more desperate than before. The King dictated a letter in response:

My father, now enemy ships are coming, and they have burnt down my towns with fire. They have done unseemly things in the land! My father is not aware that all my troops are stationed in Khatte (Hittite lands) and that all my ships are stationed in Lukka (in the Aegean). They still have not arrived, and the country is lying open like that! My father should know these things. Now the seven enemy ships that are approaching have done evil to us.

Clearly, King Ammurabi was not pleased. Thut-Moses suspected the king was still dealing with the dark shadows of the Seer's grotto from the other night and had scant reserve of patience at this point.

****

Ammurabi conferred with Thut- Moses: "The city is doomed, like the seer said. Like the prophet said. Like the astrologer said, for that matter—the day the sun was being attacked." Thut-Moses thought the king looked stricken, as he pronounced this judgement. "I am not going to call a meeting of the council. I do not have the patience for their dithering. I think it is time to evacuate the city."

Thut-Moses said, "Gibor-El, he is captain of the Guards, he can organize an evacuation plan."

"I am afraid the foreigners will be here by morning," said the King. "We need to get the women and children out of here by first light tomorrow. I am afraid we will hear the cursed horns blaring by that point."

Thut-Moses said, "I agree, sire. We can ask Gibor-El to come immediately to the throne room. He is guarding the east gate. We can get him here quickly."

They sent a messenger to fetch Gibor-El. While they waited, Thut-Moses said to the King: "Sire, I think you need to flee the city as well."

The King said, "How can I leave the city? When it is in danger?"

"You must leave, sire, and quickly. We cannot risk your life. If the city somehow survives, we need a king. Otherwise, it is chaos. And I am sure that Gibor-El would say the same. He cannot divert guards to protect you in an assault. He does not have enough men."

"We can ask Gibor-El's advice. Perhaps use the under ground passage, that goes past the granaries and to an exit beyond the wall. It will take you safely from the palace to the woods beyond, where the stables are located. You and your attendants and your guards."

****

Gibor-el and an Evacuation Plan

Gibor-El quickly joined them in the throne room. The King said, "Enemy ships are in the waters nearby! They have already attacked and burnt two towns. Cyprus and Carchemesh have both failed to send reinforcements. The enemy has skilled sailors and warriors. They will be heading to Ugarit. We have treasures that they want – the gold, the silver. We think they will be here by morning."

"What I need, Gibor-El, is your counsel. A plan to evacuate the city, to get the women and children to safety."

Gibor-El pondered for a few moments. He replied: "We should send out warnings immediately. Not waste any time. Send out messengers to the compounds in the city and tell the citizens to pack up their valuables and what-not and prepare to evacuate."

Gibor-El continued: "I can mobilize the Guards to organize the exit route. Have the refugees meet at the east gate. And hope the foreign ships give us enough time to do this.

Gibor-El went on, "We need to get you out of the city, my lord. You need to leave tonight. Depending on how long it takes to get things organized, it may have to be first thing in the morning. It would be dangerous to use the obvious exit, the North Gate. Perhaps the underground passage, my lord?"

"That is what Thut-Moses said."

"You will need a litter with porters. Donkeys to carry your bags. Thank goodness the Queens and the children have already left. You will need at least four guards. Take the road to the garrison, the guard post to the east. . It is one days' travel. If you stay there for three days, then I can get word to you. Can tell you if the city still stands. From there, you can continue to your mountain retreat if needed, my liege. If the roads are still safe."

The King said, "Go. I give you leave to organize this." Gibor-El left, to gather up the guards and to organize an evacuation.

****

The King said, "Thut-Moses, what are your plans?"

"I will stay and help defend the walls. I am an archer. I can be of use on the battlements. I will surrender if necessary. If and when the walls are overtaken. I suspect these marauders take captives and sell them off at the next port of call, as slaves."

"And where do you propose to go, if you are taken captive?"

"I hope to go to Tyre, my liege. If the city is still standing. The emissary from Tyre, he said I was welcome to come to their court, that they need a scribe."

"Good," says the King. "If the gods allow it, I will send a letter to the king in Tyre. After all this mayhem settles down and after the roads are safe. Go with my blessings. You have been a good friend." And the two men hugged. A manly hug. And parted ways. The King to start packing and preparing for a flight along the underground passage leading to the woods beyond the walls of the palace. His bard David would travel with him. Thut-Moses would help prepare for the defense of the city walls. Each to an uncertain future.

Evacuation Plan

The plan was made. Warnings went out that very evening, that enemy ships were nearby; that people should pack their things and be ready to flee if the signal is given. To take what they could carry with them. The citizenry should go to the east gate; the King's Guard would guide them rough the narrow streets to the gate and then help them as they set up camp on the highway heading east.

They could return to the city if it were safe. If not, they would have to seek shelter with relatives or friends in the outlying towns. Or in Hamath or Damascus, some distance inland. Able-bodied men would be asked to take up lance or spear and to fend off any attackers as best they could. To give the women and children more time to flee.

CHAPTER 26: PREPARING FOR AN ATTACK ON THE CITY

At the Healer's

It was almost dark by the time Menelaus came home. Yoninah saw the pallor of his face and asked: "What is it? What has happened?" He replied: "Enemy ships have attacked and burnt down nearby towns. Reports came into the harbor at noon or so. The foreman closed the harbor and told us to go home and start packing. He sent Tahir and me to the Palace to inform the King. We just got back from the palace. We spoke with Thut-Moses, the scribe, and then with the king himself. All sorts of plans are underway, to evacuate the city. We are expecting an imminent attack on Ugarit itself."

Menelaus looked unsteady as he said all this. He sat down, to settle his nerves.

It took a few breaths for Yoninah to process what Menelaus had said. Her world was turned upside down. The ground felt unsteady under her feet. She sat down as well.

She said, "We have to leave Ugarit?" "Yes," said Menelaus. The attack is expected tomorrow morning. We need to pack tonight and get ready to evacuate the city by first light."

She did not know if she would burst into tears or collapse in a heap on the floor or start picking up the pieces of her life in Ugarit and packing it into travel-size bags. She chose the latter.

Yoninah started gathering up her medicinal plants and supplies. She started collecting extra tunics and cloaks for herself and the girls. She also packed her household gods-- these were small and lightweight. Everything went into leather bags they could carry.

The girls were privy to this scene between Yoninah and Menelaus. They too started packing. She told them to pack up their treasures and extra clothes.

In the case of Bat-El, those were her figures of a camel and an elephant. In the case of Laylah, those were her gold chains, kohl, and perfume jar. Giving them sturdy leather bags in which to carry their things, Yonina told them to pack extra clothes and blankets.

Menelaus said, "As for my things, I always have a pack ready to go. A habit left over from my years as a soldier. I have a flint with which to start fires, waterbags, a tent, a rope, and other sundries. I can put a change of clothes in there and blankets as well. Ideally, I would have a spear or javelin as well. In the army, we would have a supply train, with foodstuff. Lacking that, we will need to bring some rations with us."

Yoninah said: "I can round up cheeses and dried dates from my larder. I have some breads already baked. I can pack grain and olive oil to make flatbreads on the way. I have already packed cloaks and clothes."

"What about Tahir?" Laylah protested. "He should come with us! "

"Of course, he will come with us. I have already told him to pack his gear and bring it to the house." Menelaus said. He almost smiled at her concern for Tahir.

When the girls were out of earshot, Menelaus told Yoninah that he and Tahir would have to stay behind, to help the King's Guard set up defenses, to try to hold the walls as long as possible if there were an attack. To gain time for the civilians to flee. She and the girls would have to carry Menelaus' and Tahir's packs. They would also have to keep the dog with them. If there were an attack, the dog would be a hazard in the midst of a sword fight. And to leave without the men in the morning and to wait for them in the camp outside the East Gate.

Menelaus told her: "If the city falls, and if we need to seek refuge elsewhere…My son, he can take us in. He lives five or so days from here, in Ur-Kataan, a small town in the mountains. All of us. Including that reprobate Tahir. If I do not make it back quickly from the fighting…here is a map for you and the girls to follow." He handed her a pot sherd on which he had crudely drawn, in black ink, a map. Showing the main road, leading to Hamath, and the turn off for the donkey trail that led to a small town along the river. He also gave her the bag of silver shekels that the king's scribe had given him. He said, "If I do not come back from the fighting, you and girls should go on to Ur-Kataan. I will meet you there."

She said nothing. But she gave him a hug. And said, "You had better come back from the fighting, or I will be very angry."

Menelaus hesitated for a minute. Then he said, "Here is my signet ring. With this token, I believe we are married. Show this to my son when you get to Ur-Kataan."

Yoninah took the ring. It was heavy in her hand. Made of bronze, with the Mycenean lion incised into it. She said, "I would much rather have you next to me. But thank for the betrothal and marriage, all in one fell swoop." As she looked at him, with both tears and a smile.

"Good, then that's taken care of," he said briskly and headed off to start packing up his gear.

Bat-El went to visit her friend Gedalyah next door. She had to tell him that they were packing, they had to be ready to leave in the morning. She told him and his grandmother that they should start packing too. She could not imagine leaving Gedalyah behind.

Gedalyah, as a student at the scribal school, was eager to protect his wax tablets, papyri, and stylus reeds. They were his most valuable possessions. Grandmother was less impressed. She thought they were overreacting. Gedalyah packed for his grandmother, whether she wanted him to or not.

****

That evening, after he had packed his kit, Menelaus asked Yoninah: "Are you all right?" She had said few words to him that evening.

She said, "I knew in my heart that this was coming. I have seen the city streets. They are more than half-empty. Many houses have already emptied out. People have been quietly leaving for weeks."

"We have heard the rumors," she added. "We knew that enemy ships are in the waters near Cyprus. This should be no surprise."

"But it is still hard," she said. I have lived here for thirty-three years. My children were born here. I have loved ones buried in the tombs below, the shrine to the captain is there as well. My roots go deep in Ugarit.".

And, with that, Menelaus gave her a hug. He held her for a while. He said gently: "You can explain to your mother, your captain, and the baby that you and the girls need to leave. They will understand."

Yoninah smiled a wry smile. She knew he was trying to comfort her. "I am all right. I can leave if we have no choice," she said.

The Vaulted Tomb Room

Carrying a torch for light, Yoninah visited the tombs that night. Laylah and Bat-El went with her.. Yoninah gave the deceased what gifts she had: flowers, wine, amulets. She spoke to the captain, her mother, and the baby. She wished them a peaceful time in the afterlife. She told them she might have to leave the city. If she did, she would say prayers for them wherever her journey took her and make offerings to the gods on their behalf.

Laylah and Bat-El stood close to their mother as she spoke with the dead. They both understood that something momentous was happening. They also said their goodbyes to their father and grandmother and the baby boy they had never known. They said a prayer as well: That the gods would protect their loved ones in the afterlife and would protect them as well, on their upcoming travels.

Tahir and his dog came to the house. He left a bag behind and a dog. Then he and Menelaus left for their station on the battlements. To defend the Palace Wall from attack. They were told to sleep in the Gate House. That night, Bat-El kept watch on the dog. They settled down together on her sleeping mat. She had to latch the door to keep the dog from seeking out Tahir. But she succeeded: both of them fell asleep.

****

At the Palace

That night, Thut-Moses sought solace in a few hours of sleep. Before reporting to the battlements, first thing in the morning. His dreams were restless. He and Donitaya had talked about Anat, the fierce warrior-goddess. In a vivid, disquieting dream, Anat made a fearsome appearance. She wore heads of slain warriors on her belt and waded through the blood of men she had killed. She wore henna on her hair, kohl on her eyes, red on her lips. She was both beautiful and frightening.

In the wont of dream-images, she transmuted into the Egyptian goddess Sekhmet. With the body of a woman and head of a lioness. The Egyptian goddess of war. She continued to wade in pools of blood. The dream was terrifying enough that he woke up. Which was just as well. It was before first light, and he needed to get to the Guard Tower.

PART 3: SOUNDING OF THE HORNS AND THE DAYS AFTER

When an enemy approaches the city wall…If the watchman on the tower sees the sword approaching against the country, and he blows the horn and warns the people…. If anybody hears the horn but ignores the warning, and the sword comes and dispatches him, his blood shall be on his own head. Since he heard the horn, but ignored the warning, his blood guilt shall be upon himself; had he taken the warning, he would have saved his life.

--From the Book of Ezekiel

CHAPTER 27: FLIGHT

At the house on Palace Street, Yoninah and the household arose at first light. They had hardly slept the night before, what with anticipating an imminent flight from the city.

As the faint light of early morning filtered in through their window slits, Yoninah and the girls heard seven blasts of the rams' horns. That was the signal: "Enemy ships sighted by the lookouts on the Temple Tower." Time was of the essence. They grabbed their bags and Menelaus' and Taj's bags and fled into the street. The dog was on a leash. Bat-El navigated her nimbly through the streets. Neighbors appeared, looking confused and scared. Gedalyah and grandmother spotted Yoninah and the girls and followed them, as they ran towards the eastern gate. Guards showed them which street to take and urged them on.

Just like in her dream, there were arrows flying overhead: enemy archers shooting into the city, to frighten them. The tactic was effective—they were afraid. Some arrows were on fire. Yoninah's cloak caught an ember and started to burn. She quickly dropped her bags and shed her cloak. A searing pain ran along her back. She found she could ignore the pain. She grabbed her bags again and found her daughters, who had walked a short distance ahead of her.

She took them by the hand and pulled them forward, away from the flying embers. Her breath caught in her throat. Smoke from small fires surrounded them. Her eyes focused on the next Guard along the street. He signaled them to the gate, which they made in record time. She collapsed just outside the city walls. The flying, burning arrows did not have sufficient range to reach the eastern city gate. She breathed a sigh of relief for this small piece of refuge. The guards signaled them to go on, another 100 paces, to a patch of trees and pastures. They were told to make camp.

She told Laylah to go through her bags, to find the ointment with opium and myrrh and to apply it to her burns. Laylah did so. "The skin is red but not blistering," said Laylah Lack of blisters was a good sign. She also knew pain was a good sign. A deep burn did not hurt. A superficial one did. After a few minutes, the salve eased the pain.

CHAPTER 28: DEFENSE OF THE PALACE GATE

Before First Light

Thut-Moses had volunteered his services as an archer, at the defense of the Palace Gate. Before sunrise, Gibor-El and Thut-Moses stood ready at the Guardhouse. Another twenty men from the King's Guard joined them, as well as ten men from the city.

Thut-Moses recognized one of the King's Guards, the man he would run into on the occasional nights he would return to the palace after an evening spent at the harbor bar. The guard was an older man with the weathered expression of a retired soldier. He always pretended he did not recognize Thut-Moses and Tahir. But he would be gracious if a handsome woman presented for admission to the gates.

The Guard Tower rose ten cubits above the road, providing a height advantage over any attackers. Besides the advantage of height, weapons at the ready included throwing spears, slings, bows and arrows, and rocks. The plan was to send volleys of arrows once the enemy forces were within range; to aim bronze-tipped spears at them, and to drop rocks on their heads as they stood directly below the Tower.

Gibor-El gave a short speech in a booming voice.

"We are here to defend the Palace walls. We will be outnumbered. Our goal is to slow down the attack long enough that the citizens and the King can flee. When the gate is taken, we are to retreat."

"Is the King safe?" a man called out after the speech.

"We asked him to leave the city, to wait and see how things fare," Gibor-El said. "If the city stands, we will need him to return. He should be on his way to a fortified retreat as we speak."

"And David the bard?" asked Thut-Moses. "Is he safe as well?"

"He left with the King," Gibor-El replied.

Thut-Moses felt relieved. He looked over the men gathered on the Tower. He recognized Menelaus, the Mycenean who had the day before brought word of attacks on nearby towns. The man was holding a spear and shield, handling his weapons well. He was evidently a trained soldier. The younger man with him, the same man from the day before, also handled his weapons well. The younger man held a lance in one hand, with a dagger in his belt as backup.

****

At the first rays of the morning sun lightened the sky, the soldiers heard the warning: the blaring of the horns. The lookouts on the temple tower had spotted the ships of the enemy approaching the harbor.

The men took their stations, preparing for an assault on the walls. They were prepared to fight until the walls fell, but they did not foresee how rapid it would be.

The marauders had swiftly beached their shallow draught ships. They had offloaded their warriors on the beach. The blast of horns was still ongoing, and the attackers had already massed at the gate of the lower city, the closest to their landing on the beach.

Within a short time, the invaders took the lower city and were at the Palace ramparts. The early morning light showed a mass of foreigners that would be impossible to defeat. To Thut-

Moses' eyes, they were tall, these foreigners, wearing helmets decorated with horns or feathers, carrying double-edged swords and leather shields. An impressive number of them, well over one hundred, with more arriving even as he watched.

As the enemy approached, Gibor-El gave the signal to the archers to let fly their arrows. Thut-Moses was among the group of archers. He had learned the skill as a boy in his native Nubia. His eyes were good, his aim unflinching. He took down two of the attackers: an arrow to the shoulder of one, an arrow to the back of another.

The enemy archers returned volleys of arrows. The man next to Thut-Moses –the gruff guard from the palace gate--was struck by an arrow to the chest. He collapsed and toppled backwards over the top of the battlements. He fell heavily onto the stone courtyard of the palace. As his head hit the stones of the courtyard, Thut-Moses heard a loud cracking. The man thrashed around momentarily and then was still.

Thut-Moses could see blood oozing out on the stones. The gruesome scene reminded him of the medical papyrus that he had read with Queen Donitaya. The first patient, the one that upset the Queen. He had time to recollect this stray memory and wished he had not seen it. He turned back to the battle in front of him and took up his bow and strung a fresh arrow. With a surge of fear, he remained on high alert.

Another volley of enemy arrows flew over the parapet. This time, an arrow struck Thut-Moses in the chest. He crumpled to the ground from the force of the arrow. Thut-Moses was momentarily stunned. After a short span of time, he opened his eyes again and saw that Menelaus was bending over him, opening his tunic.

"Your bronze amulet has taken the blow," Menelaus said. "You are lucky. You will have a bruise, but the flesh is otherwise uninjured."

Thut-Moses quickly regained his wits and his breath He got back to his feet. The eunuch gave silent thanks to Isis his protector. And to his short acquaintance with the healer who had given him the amulet.

Meanwhile, the men on the battlements were bombarding the foreigners with their throwing spears. Menelaus sent a sharp-tipped spear into their midst and then got another one from a cache on the Tower to replace it. Other men also sent spears or threw rocks into the soldiers below.

The engagement continued, with the attackers staying in formation below. Then two men among the foreigners were spotted carrying large, sharp bronze axes. The men on top of the ramparts could hear and feel the heavy blows on the thick wood of the heavy wooden gate reinforced with bronze. Then they heard a great cracking sound. The door was splitting.

At this point, Gibor-El told his men to halt.

"The door is taken!" Gibor-El shouted. "The lower city has fallen. The upper city will fall as well."

Gibor-El ordered the herald to sound an alarm. A series of long and short blasts warned anyone still in the streets to run. The alarm also warned the men offering a defense to the attacking forces to retreat and run for the east gate.

"Retreat! Do not play the hero and stay here to die!" Gibor-El said.

The men under his command did not argue. They quickly grabbed their spears and other weapons and made their way down the stairs and into the plaza inside the walls of the palace.

Thut-Moses got caught up in the crowd of men dashing down the stairs, down from the tower to the courtyard below. He found himself in a group of Ugaritic men at the base of the stairs. The Mycenean and his young friend joined him and the three formed a cohort. The enemy soldiers were already pouring in through the shattered gate.

A young man, a volunteer from the city, caught the blade raised by one of the fierce sea raiders. He went down in a pool of blood. Again, not a scene that Thut-Moses relished.

"May the gods help him find his way to the underworld." Menelaus said a prayer for the fallen youth.

The three of them – Thut-Moses, Menelaus, and his Afghani friend – fought as a unit, as they cut their way through the crowd of enemy warriors at the base of the Guard Tower. To Thut-Moses' estimation, everything became a blur of swords, spears, and shields. He saw the Afghani deftly block adversaries with the shaft of his lance.

"Thank the gods for this young man," Thut-Moses thought to himself. "His reflexes are sharp. He turns quickly to confront anyone approaching our position."

Thut-Moses saw the young man take a cut to his arm and keep going.

The three men fought their way out of the throng of enemies and broke free and headed to the east. As they ran through the maze of streets that led towards the gate in the lower city, there was a second and then a third episode of hand-to-hand fighting. In these close quarters, Thut-Moses' skills as an archer were of minimal use. But Menelaus and the Afghani got them away with deft moves of thrusting spears and nimble footwork.

The mid-day sun beat down on the three of them, the sweat pouring off their foreheads. Thut-Moses, from the advantage of his height, spotted a squad of enemy soldiers about to top a rise just below their position. He said as much to Menelaus and the young Afghani.

"On their way to join their friends, to finish looting and torching the city," the young man said darkly.

Thut-Moses quickly drew his bow and fitted an arrow to it. He took careful aim at the lead soldier, who was still a good distance away and unaware of their presence. Thut-Moses let the arrow fly with a satisfying hiss. The arrow caught the lead solider on the right shoulder. The solider fell, but it was not a mortal wound. But he was taken out of action.

When the remaining soldiers spied the men from Ugarit, the second in line drew a sword. Raising his shield to his chest, he came rushing at them. Thut-Moses saw Menelaus lift his throwing spear and take aim. He caught the man with his bronze tipped spear at an unprotected spot on just below the margin of the chest shield. The spear tip slowed him down. He fell to the ground. A pool of blood blossomed around him.

The third man in line lifted his sword and shield and rushed towards Menelaus.

"Menelaus is defenseless, his spear is spent," Thut-Moses thought to himself. Thee eunuch rapidly notched a fresh arrow and sent it flying. The arrow caught the would-be attacker in the chest. The shield protected him from a lethal injury. But the man was momentarily stunned, which gave the Afghani enough time to tackle him and drive home a dagger into his back.

The fourth man in the group took off running after he saw his comrades fall.

"God-speed to him," thought Thut-Moses. He did not relish the thought of a further engagement.

Thut-Moses watched as Menelaus pulled his spear from the dead man's gut. There was scant time to celebrate any victory, however. Another squad of attackers was heading their way, from the harbor towards the palace gate.

Thut-Moses spotted them and decided it was enough. He had seen enough pools of blood this day. Mostly men from Ugarit, lying dead in the streets; some from slain enemy soldiers. Each scarlet pool reminded him of Anat/Shekset and her endless delight in blood.

He signaled to his compatriots to go ahead without him. Menelaus and the youth did not linger. They turned sharply and took a different road towards the east.

As the soldiers approached, with raised swords and fierce expressions on their faces, Thut-Moses dramatically put his bow and arrows on the ground. He lifted both arms above his head in clear surrender. He started reciting in the language he spoke as a child.

"Better a live dog than a dead lion," Thut-Moses said in Nubian. His father had taught him this when he was a boy.

The enemy soldiers were taken aback. Just before they got to him, the ground shook. Evidently another tremor. Either they were unfamiliar with tremors, or they were superstitious about the sight of a tall black man with his arms raised to heaven who was reciting an incantation in an unknown language.

In any event, they paused in their approach. More gently than Thut-Moses expected, they took him captive. Thut-Moses prayed that they would lead him away to their ships. Thut-Moses hoped to live long enough to once again pick up a stylus and a scroll; to once again scribe for a royal house. For right now, though, he would bide his time.

CHAPTER 29: OUTSIDE THE CITY

The Women and Children Wait

A safe distance from the east gate, underneath the shade of a cypress tree, Yoninah had put down her bags and the girls' bags. Bat-El, with the dog in tow, had settled gratefully onto the patch of rough grasses underneath the tree's branches. Laylah also sat. They were all still short of breath from the race to the east gate. The guards had given them beer and bread. Gedalyah and grandmother and others fleeing the city had also joined them under the sheltering tree. With the late morning sun beating down, they had all appreciated the shade.

By early afternoon, with a wind blowing from the west, they had smelled smoke: the scent of burning wood and buildings on fire. They could hear the distant sounds of swords clashing and of men's voices raised in combat. With unintelligible gutturals mixed with Semitic sibilants.

Yoninah and her daughters had sought a vantage point.

Climbing a rock nearby and looking down on the city to the west, they could see the fires burning. Beyond the city, they could see the waves of the Great Sea lapping the shores.

By mid-afternoon, with the sun well beyond its noontime peak, the women and children --and it was mostly women and children encamped there---had prayed for their husbands, brothers, and sons to make it back safely to their camp.

At which point, Tahir's dog started barking wildly. Bat-El let her loose from her leash and she loped joyfully to two figures approaching from the direction of the gate. Menelaus and Tahir appeared. The dog ran to Tahir and licked him enthusiastically. The two men looked exhausted. Tahir appeared to be clutching a bloodied left arm; Menelaus appeared to be carrying a sack in the shape of a baby.

Menelaus found Yoninah under the cypress tree, in her makeshift camp. She was thrilled to see him alive. It took a few seconds before she noticed that he was indeed toting a baby around. She had her arms around him before she firmly identified a baby in his arms. She looked at him quizzically. He said: "Take the child. His mother is dead. I found him on the road to the gate. He was crying. I could not leave him there, in the road like that."

She nodded her understanding. She took the child from him. She was herself traumatized by their flight from the city. And the loss of her house. She knew her arms did not take the child gracefully. Her heart was too numb. But she took him. Bat-El stood next to her. She said, "Let me hold him, mother. You look tired." And Bat-El took him from her mother. "Thank you, dear," said Yoninah to her daughter. She was grateful to her. The day had been too much for Yoninah.

Yoninah looked at Tahir's wound: a goodly gash, of more than a finger length, deep enough to require stitching. She commissioned Laylah to wash the wound and to find the needle, thread, and numbing medicine from her healer's bag. She knew Laylah was skilled in suturing. She had done it before, for the walking wounded in Ugarit.

Tahir was happy to see the family. He was less than enthusiastic about a sewing project on his arm. But he allowed Laylah to do the job. She poured watered down wine on the wound afterwards. She wrapped it in clean dressings. Tahir grimaced when she applied the dressing. She told him: "Don't be a baby. It doesn't hurt that bad."

Yoninah and the girls fed Menelaus and Tahir bread and beer from the common food stores. Bat-El held the baby and fed him a spoonful of bread soaked in beer. He took this offer without complaint. Besides being overwhelmed by his new surroundings, he was also hungry.

When they were rested and Tahir's wound was bandaged, they sat around a circle on the ground. Menelaus told them about the battle for the city.

"The city is gone. The foreigners torched it. Nothing is left except for ashes," said Menelaus.

"First, they looted it, taking what valuables they could find. They took some stores of grain and wine. What they mostly wanted was the gold and silver in the Temples and in the Palace. We barely escaped with our lives. The foreigners carried these ungodly swords: long and double-edged. They can slash through a man before he knows it."

"How did they take the city so quickly?" asked Gedalyah's grandmother.

"They easily breached the walls of the lower city. We had few defenders there and the walls were weakened already. They rampaged through the lower city, with scant resistance. Their goal was always the palace and temple compounds. The upper city. That's where the King's Guard and the we civilians were stationed, at the Guard Tower of the upper city. Maybe thirty defenders, all told."

"We resisted as best we could. I had throwing spears to send into their mass. Tahir threw rocks from over the edge of the battlements. Crushed a few heads. Thut-Moses – the king's scribe and aide—he was there. Turns out he is a skilled archer. He took out a few of their number. But we were outmatched. They had over a hundred soldiers.

And they had a whole phalanx of skilled archers who sent arrows into our midst. They got a few of our men. Thut-Moses caught an arrow in the chest. We thought he was dead. Turns out, the arrow struck a bronze amulet he was wearing. He was knocked out for a bit but was otherwise all right."

"I know this man!" exclaimed Yoninah. He came to the shop. I gave him that amulet. He wanted it for good luck. I am glad it saved his life!"

Menelaus nodded at her interjection and continued with his telling of the day's grim events. "In the end we were no match for the attackers. They came at the great wooden door of the Guard tower with heavy bronze axes. And made short work of smashing its enormous wooden beams. Our captain called a retreat. We ran down the staircase of the tower and into the courtyard. To a mass of enemies who had already breached the gate."

"We cut our way through, as best we could. I had my spear; Tahir had his lance and dagger. Thut-Moses stayed with us."

As we ran through the streets, we could see the houses on fire. Their thatch roofs had caught fire in the initial volley of blazing arrows from the morning. We cleared our way through a third or fourth squad of raiders. Thut-Moses taking down a few with bow and arrow. Tahir and I got away...."

"And Thut-Moses?" asked Yoninah with some trepidation.

"Thut-Moses was surrounded and raised his hands in surrender. We think he got taken to their ships as a captive."

"Oh," said Yoninah. "I like the man. I hope he is all right." She remembered his expressive face and overly-long legs. She found it hard to imagine him as a captive on an enemy ship.

"As we looked behind us, we could see upper city on fire. The attackers had set the Palace and Temple Mount on fire..."

"The men who fell during the fighting... the fire probably did them in. I am so sorry for the widows and orphans." Menelaus' voice cracked. And he suddenly looked exhausted, thought Yoninah.

After a momentary pause, Gedalyah's grandmother asked: "What about the king and the court?"

"We think they escaped," said Menelaus. "The King and his attendants."

"Ah, that is good," said the grandmother. She continued: "What happens to us now? Is there any city to city to go back to?" Her voice was unsteady. That was the question on everyone's mind.

"In the morning, when the fires have burnt down, the King's Guard will send men to survey what remains of the city. If enough is left standing, we can rebuild. In my opinion, I think the city is gone and we need to think about seeking refuge elsewhere."

"As for me and Tahir, we are just thrilled to see you all. What happens tomorrow or the next week, we will deal with it," Menelaus concluded.

****

As evening came on, the refugees ate what bread, cheese, and figs they had. They drank what beer was available. The guards gave them food from the stores they had brought.

Bat-El fed the baby bread soaked in beer. She also gave him mashed-up dates. The child took the dates avidly. He had to gum everything to death. He was barely a year old; his teeth had not come in yet. He looked at his new companions with wide eyes. He was not altogether happy about his new situation. None of them were, for that matter. They slept that night on the hard ground, covered with blankets for warmth. The guards said not to build fires, not until they knew the foreign invaders were gone. Bat-El wrapped the child in a blanket and slept with him next to her, to keep him warm.

Yoninah knew that she was not yet ready to take care of the baby. What with the loss of her house, she felt like a shadow of herself. That night, Menelaus lay next to her and told her more details about his and Tahir's flight from the city.

She knew he had scars from his years as a soldier. She knew that he was skilled and had no doubt handled himself well in the day's combat. She also knew that revisiting scenes of death and dying cost him dearly. She gave him a hug, as they lay in their nest of blankets and cloaks.

With sounds of mourning throughout the camp. The children crying, the women weeping for sons and husbands who had failed to return from the city. Eventually the camp grew quiet, and the refugees slept. This was their first night in exile. They did not know yet if it would be their last.

CHAPTER 30: SWEEP OF THE BURNT CITY

The next morning, the King's Guard re-entered what remained of the city. They drafted Menelaus and Tahir to accompany them.

There was smoke everywhere. They found that most walls had collapsed, what with the torching of the wooden supports that held up the roofs. The destruction went far beyond what they had expected. They knew that some people had hidden their gold and treasures in their houses, anticipating a quick return to the city. The degree of destruction was such that any hiding places were buried under feet of rubble. They doubted that any treasures would be recovered.

They did find four survivors, amidst the rubble. The first man they found was in the pool in the palace courtyard. He had survived the inferno by sheltering in the pool overnight. He was wet and cold and kept saying: "Thank the gods!"

The next two men they found were injured but could walk with assistance. The fourth man had a broken leg and required a sled to carry him. They got all four of them to the east gate and to the camp of refugees. Yoninah in the camp set the broken leg. She had packed a splint and linen dressings in her travel bag. She gave the man pain medicine – ground poppy seed mixed into beer– for the pain.

The attackers must have already rounded up their dead and wounded. They found no evidence of the soldiers wearing the distinctive kilts and facial hair of the enemy.

Tahir looked for any treasure he could pick up. He was still a street urchin at heart. He came across two bowls and a bronze statuette that the homeowners or the pillagers had dropped. He packed these up in a sack he had found. He had to protect his left arm, though; the one that had been sliced in the defense of the city.

Menelaus scavenged in the ruins as well and found bronze daggers for the taking. Also, an abandoned bow, with arrows in the quiver. He also found a stray goat that had somehow survived the destruction of the city. He picked it up. He found a rope and made a tether for it.

The King's Guard, with Menelaus and Tahir to help them, finished their survey of the ruined city. At the end of a long day, the men and a goat headed to the camp just outside the east gate. A crowd of hundreds of unhappy anxious people awaited them.

The King's Guard demanded order in the camp. "Now, listen up! We need quiet. We have an official judgement to declare!"

The crowd of refugees settled down. The King's Guard confirmed that the city had been leveled. "In our official judgement, the city is gone. All of us need to continue trekking to the east, along the highway to Hamath. We need to get over the mountains and head towards Damascus. We need to put distance between us and the sea. To get away from these marauders."

The people took these words under consideration. Some burst into tears at the news that they would not be going home again. Others started setting up camp for the oncoming night. The mass of people ate a dinner of sorts, provided again by the Guards. Someone passed around dried cheeses.

The recently rescued young man who had sheltered in the pool overnight had recovered enough to tell them the tale of his ordeal. As they listened to his story, Yoninah whispered to Menelaus: "He looks so slender and pale. It was a miracle that he had the stamina to survive."

Jeru-Baal's Story/The Man in the Pool

"I was scribe to Urtenu, at his grand house near the palace. I was still packing up scrolls and other things when I heard the blasts of the rams' horns, just after first light of morning."

The young man took a deep breath and continued his story.

"The next several minutes were chaotic. It took me a few moments to finish packing. I heard shouts in the street. I ran outside. The street was packed with people, all trying to head to the east gate. I turned right, towards the palace itself. My goal being the underground passage-Urtenu had told me to head there—to gain safe passage to the woods beyond the city wall. "

Here the listeners paid close attention, the young people especially. Gedalyah looked worried for the young scribe.

"I gained entry to the Palace grounds by a secret gate towards the margin of the Courtyard, " Jeru-Baal continued. "I could hear commotion behind me: the clashing of swords, the ping of spears as they bounced off shields, the shouts of men.

the hiss of arrows flying overhead. Clearly, the Guard Tower of the Palace gate was already under attack."

He took another deep breath before continuing his story.

"I ran across the courtyard and towards the east wing of the palace. The door into the place was left agape and I slipped in. The soldiers were clearly about to breach the south gate and spill into the courtyard. I heard the horns begin to sound: the wall was indeed breached. "

"What did you do then?" asked Gedalyah, with concern in his young voice.

 "In front of me stood a grand staircase which I quickly climbed. It led into a suite of rooms – probably the Queen's apartment, I thought. In niches along the wall were giant decorated pots planted with papyrus shoots. 'Looks like a good hiding place,' I thought. Moving a heavy pot a short distance from the wall, I crouched down behind it and pulled it back into position. Hiding deep in the niche in the wall, I was grateful I was slender and could fit."

After a short pause, Jeru-Baal continued: "Soon I heard the heavy footfalls of enemy soldiers in the palace and in the suite itself. Heavy voices of one man shouting to another in a foreign language. I held my breath. They apparently grabbed whatever gold or bronze treasures they could. I stayed hidden until I heard them leave. Which seemed to take an eternity. When the peace and quiet held for a brief span of time, I peeked out from my hiding place. No sign of life in the room outside. I breathed a sigh of relief. And instantly smelled smoke. The enemy had set the Palace on fire, as they made their way out. Fires were rising everywhere."

Again the young scribe paused in his recitation. He seemed to gather what strength he had, to finish the story. "Dodging the fires, I made it out the door, to the Great Courtyard below. By this time, the walls of the palace were ablaze. The wooden beams that supported the upper stories had eagerly caught fire. I spotted the pool in the middle of the Courtyard : far enough from the burning building to offer some refuge. In a desperate sprint across the Courtyard, I made it to the pool. And quickly submerged as best I could, while embers flew across the Great Courtyard."

Gedalayah and the rest of the audience could appreciate his dilemma. They took had fled the city through a hail of burning embers.

"I stayed there through the day as the city burned around me. I stayed there through the night. The fountain that fed the pool thankfully brought fresh cool water from its source, outside the city wall. For this I was grateful. I spent the night reciting whatever prayers I could remember."

Jeru-Baal was silent for a beat, then continued: "When the sun rose the next morning, the fires were dying out. The grand wooden columns of the palace grounds were toppled and still burning. The stone foundations of the ground floor still stood, but the upper stories – built of mudbrick supported by wood beams, they were reduced to ashes. But I had survived. Tired and wet and cold but nonetheless alive. I was thankful to the men who found me and pulled me out of the water. "

At this, Yoninah saw Jeru-Baal smile at Menelaus and Tahir. A tired smile, but a smile nonetheless. She was heartened at this young man's display of courage and of endurance.

****

As Jeru-Baal told his harrowing tale of survival in the midst of a raging fire, his listeners felt sorry for the young man. Menelaus gave him a dry tunic to wear and a cloak for warmth. They told him to stay with them in their sleeping circle. Gedalyah took his hand and led him to a spot in their circle.

The camp got ready for sleep. The refugees on the road placed their cloaks and blankets on the ground again.

At their makeshift camp under the boughs of the cypress tree, Tahir managed to milk the goat they had captured. Bat-El prepared a mash of bread and fresh goat milk. The baby took the mash eagerly. Again, Bat-El wrapped the child in a blanket and slept next to him. And Yoninah and her group finally fell asleep as well. It had been an eventful day.

PART 4: ON THE ROAD

The gods sent raiders from the sea…. The enemy advanced like a great storm roaring over the earth, a devastating flood that leveled everything. Wielding bronze axes, large bows, barbed arrows, and deadly swords, they breeched the great gates, the great walls. They set the city to the torch and left it as ashes. The people were afraid. Those who had not been felled by weapons, they fled. Women and children fled to the countryside. They were given over to life as exiles, far from their beloved city.

--Adapted from "Lament for Ur" (Coogan 2013)

CHAPTER 31: ON THE ROAD
TO HAMATH

Early the next morning, the camp of refugees began their trek. The morning was cooler because they were in the mountains now. They were no longer sweltering in the summer heat of a city by the sea.

Before they set out, Menelaus made a sling for the baby. Laylah offered to carry him on her back. She was stronger than Bat-El.

The group of them made quite a sight, Yoninah thought to herself. Bat-El led the goat while Laylah carried the baby. Gedalyah and his grandmother tagged along behind the girls, with Menelaus, Tahir and his dog bringing up the rear. The young scribe rescued from the pool in Ugarit also traveled with them.

Yoninah could tell that Menelaus and Tahir, with years of experience of life on the road, greeted the day with muted enthusiasm. They almost looked forward to the coming adventure. One had been a soldier for ten years, the other a caravan driver. They knew about surviving on the road.

She knew that Menelaus had seen cities burn before. As a soldier in Troy, he had seen civilians slaughtered or sold off to slavery.

"The loss of Ugarit is not as disastrous as what befell Troy," Menelaus had said to Yoninah the night before. "The city is leveled, that is true. But most of the citizenry have escaped. No wholesale slaughter, no wholesale taking of men and women as slaves to be sold at their next opportunity."

Tahir was also sanguine about being back on the road. "I know this road," Tahir called out as they started their journey. "The road to Hamath. I have traveled it on donkey caravans."

Yoninah wished she had Tahir's confidence. She had never seen a city leveled before. She had never traveled on a road as a refugee. Feeling like she was being torn in two, she sorely missed her house, with its thick walls and solid doors.

She remembered a lament she had heard as a child when refugees from a ruined city in Sumeria, to the east, had settled in Ugarit. The refugee women would sit in the street and mourn for the homes they had lost.

"This my house, where good food is no longer eaten, where good drink is no longer drunk,.. where good beds are no longer slept in….my house, in which I dwell no more."

While she recited these words from a childhood memory under her breath, she felt too traumatized to deeply miss the city. She could still recall the sounds and screams of the burning city they had left behind.

The King's Guard guided them further east, away from the ruined city. The flood of refugees numbered about five hundred. They made up a motley crew. Mostly from the lower city, they included prostitutes, shopkeepers, dockworkers, and sailors caught up in the events of the day.

The wealthy folk who lived in the upper city must have fled some other way. The denizens of the palace compound – including the King and his court— must have headed to the north side of the city and taken a different road to get to their mountain sanctuaries.

The road to Hamath was pounded flat with years of foot and cart traffic. The rainy season was over, and the road was dry and dusty. The road was wide enough for five people to walk abreast. The King's men provided security of sorts. Spears and lances at the ready, they stood alongside the road. prepared to intervene if any brawls broke out. Or if any bandits attacked.

Carrying sacks full of their worldly possessions, the ragtag crowd walked for hours as the day grew hotter. Children cried, saying they didn't want to walk anymore. Mothers carried them. Others offered to carry the children Even the occasional donkey was drafted to carry them.

By noon, the road had turned into a shimmering ribbon of heat. Yoninah's throat felt parched, the dust coating her tongue. She rested for a few minutes and took a sip of water from the waterskin they carried. The guards told them all to take a break, to shelter under the nearby trees to avoid the merciless sun. They took a modest meal and drank more water or beer. Once the sun passed its zenith and the shadows started growing longer, they resumed their trek.

There would be an occasional squirrel or wild cat along the trail. Tahir's dog would bark at whatever critter they came across. Yoninah could hear birdsong in the trees, an oddly cheerful sound. Otherwise, it was just the dusty road and the searing sun. Finally, the sun dipped below the horizon, painting the sky in hues of orange and purple.

"The smoke to the west is catching the light, making the sunset more splendid. The smoke of our burning city." Yoninah thought, as she looked at the brilliant sunset with a pang.

They made camp for the night. As they settled into a patch of ground, Yoninah felt a flicker of hope. They had survived the first day.

The guards gave them what bread and beer they still had. Yoninah had some hard cheese to share with the others. She also had some dried dates. Yoninah, biting into the date, felt a small stirring of hope. A sweet end to a terrible day.

The goat provided fresh milk for the child, who took mashed up bread and goat milk with obvious glee. The child seemed more comfortable and fell asleep quickly, as night came, lying on his makeshift bed with Laylah and Bat-El on either side.

****

A second day traveling with the horde of refugees from Ugarit – another day of dusty roads, searing sun, tired feet, and complaining children.

When they made camp that evening, just as Yoninah was falling asleep in her makeshift bed of blankets on the hard ground, an older woman came to her campsite.

"Come, help me!" cried the woman as she shook Yoninah by the shoulder. "My daughter just had a baby! And she is bleeding. I cannot stop the bleeding! Come, you are the healer, are you not? I recognized you from Palace Street."

Yoninah reluctantly climbed out of her blankets. She woke up Laylah and had her come along. Laylah found the bag of medicinal plants that included an ergot pessary. In Ugarit, Yoninah had dealt with several women bleeding after childbirth.

They followed the woman to a nearby camp. A young woman was lying down on a pallet of leaves and blankets, with a pool of blood between her legs. Yoninah, still marginally asleep, told the mother she was going to place a cloth in the birth canal.

"The medicine in which it is soaked, it should stop the bleeding," Yoninah said. She washed her hands and then placed the cloth gently a good distance in the birth canal. Meanwhile, a newborn baby girl was resting on the new mother's chest. The child was crying.

"That's a good, healthy cry," Yoninah said.

The new mother was largely unaware of her surroundings and of Yoninah's ministrations. She only moaned and turned her head to one side.

They waited. They waited some more. After a short while, the bleeding slowed and finely stopped. Yoninah gave the young mother sips of beer to drink, so she could regain her strength. The young mother mumbled a few words of thanks and asked to see her baby. And then fell asleep.

The new grandmother picked up the newborn and gently wrapped her in a blanket. She handed the baby to Laylah to hold. The grandmother tended to her daughter, cleaning up the bed and gently covering her with blankets.

"Keep giving her beer or wine or water to drink," Yoninah said. "She needs to build up her blood again."

"Can you give the child a blessing?" the grandmother asked. "To protect her at this difficult time? To protect my daughter from further harm?"

Yoninah took the baby from Laylah. Yoninah felt a surge of hope for this small family and for her own. She ascribed this surge of hope to the presence of the gods, even on this trek. Holding the child in her left arm, raising her right arm in the ritual gesture of prayer, she recited the blessing for a newborn, invoking Asherah's protection:

"May the Goddess of Heaven protect you and bless you. May she turn her face towards you. May her favor shine upon you. May she shield you from harm. May Asherah give you and your new child health and protection. And may the demons who prey on the birth couch stay far away. Amen."

"Thank you, healer," the grandmother bowed her head. She gave Yoninah in payment a bag of dried dates, the best currency she had.

"And the child's name? Do you know what you are going to name her?" Yoninah asked.

"'Bat-Oni – daughter of travail,'" replied the new grandmother. "Leaving Ugarit like that, it brought on my daughter's labor, and it was a difficult one." And the newly named Bat-Oni opened her eyes and looked at the world with eyes of wonder. Yoninah handed her back to the grandmother and said good night.

Yoninah and Laylah quickly returned to their sleeping nests. Yoninah held a vision of a newborn's face dancing before her. Even though the child's name was not an uplifting one, it was still a comforting vision as she fell back asleep.

CHAPTER 32: THE DONKEY TRAIL

On the next morning, to one side of the road to Hamath, they spotted a pile of stones marking the spot where a narrow trail intersected with the larger road.

"It's the donkey trail," said Menelaus. "It will take us to Ur-Kataan. Another four or five days from here, due north."

They said goodbye to the young scribe who had traveled with them and turned onto the narrow trail.

The path was just wide enough for a donkey carrying jars on either side. Yoninah noted its narrowness with some trepidation: the mountain side to their left, with a steep drop-off to their right. Some distance below, there was a river flowing.

"We will have to walk single file or no more than two abreast," said Yoninah.

"Don't worry," said Tahir. "I've walked on trails like this before. The bushes and small trees along the drop-off, they should stop your fall if you happen to step off the trail. I do not think you will die."

Tahir's words were not entirely comforting. They nonetheless assumed a formation, strung in a chain along the narrow path. They were able to walk with some skill. Their feet were becoming callused and hardened. Although Gedalyah's grandmother was not as nimble as the others, she nonetheless managed to keep up and not to fall.

As they started hiking, Tahir told Gedalyah about bandits on the road, from when he worked the donkey caravans crossing from Afghanistan to Mari. Gedalyah looked worried, his shoulders tense.

"Are there bandits on this trail?" Gedalyah asked. "Are we safe?"

"Don't worry, we don't carry any cargo," Tahir said. "We should take off whatever gold jewelry we are wearing. I have already taken off my necklace and earrings. If we are not wearing gaudy gold jewelry, then we look like poor, bedraggled refugees on the road. We don't even have much food on us either. If I were a bandit, I wouldn't give us a second glance." After a short pause, he added. "Not that I've ever been a bandit, mind you."

"Didn't you used to be a street urchin in Afghanistan?" Laylah asked. "Didn't you tell us you had to steal food to get by?"

"That doesn't count," Tahir said. "I've earned my keep fair and square since then."

The group fell silent after this exchange. Gedalyah seemed reassured about the danger of the bandits.

Bat-El carried packs and led the goat on a leash. Laylah carried the baby in a sling on her back. The dog kept pace with Tahir. They made a colorful group along the trail, if anyone were to see them.

They walked from sunrise until evening, with a break in the middle of the day as a respite from the summer sun.

After a while, the young people would take turns carrying the baby in the sling. Tahir of all people would sing songs to him. Yoninah wondered if these were songs his mother had taught him years ago. Or perhaps the songs were in praise of the wiles of prostitutes, songs he had learned as a young man traveling the roads. Tahir sang in a pleasant tenor, and the baby gurgled happily.

Yoninah envied the ease with which the young people took care of the child. Bat-El had taken the tending of the baby as a serious matter. She had even come up with a name for him: Nathan-El, which meant gift of God. The name was fitting. The child had appeared out of nowhere as a joyful gift for little Bat-El.

Yoninah knew she was keeping her distance from the baby. Her heart was too battered to deal with the needs of a small child, especially one who had just lost his mother. She hoped at some point she would again be able to hold a child with genuine affection and ease. But she couldn't this day, not yet.

****

They spotted another pile of stones towards evening. Down below, heading towards the river to their right, was a path that led to a small town nestled along its banks.

"There are shelters for the night, along this trail," Menelaus said. "People in the towns along the trail will let us stay in their out-buildings, with hay for the donkeys we do not have. And beds of straw for the travelers themselves. It is expected that we pay them a few shekels for the privilege of staying indoors. Which is well worth it, if you ask me. The dog and the goat can even stay with us. That is a bonus, eh?"

So they made their way down the path and found a townsman who would indeed rent them a spot in their donkey shed for a few shekels. This was a far better situation than making camp on an exposed mountain trail. They lay down their sheepskins and cloaks, to soften the straw otherwise provided for bedding. They put down their bags and got comfortable as the evening grew dark around them.

They ate dry cheeses and figs and dates for their dinner. Their host even provided some beer to drink. They fed the baby bread mixed with goat's milk, a meal which he seemed to enjoy, plus a morsel of dried fruit and a bit of cheese. Bat-El took charge of feeding the baby. She wrapped him again in a blanket and lay down next to him on their makeshift bed. She sang him a little lullaby. One that Yoninah used to sing for her. Yoninah noted this display of maternal behavior. She still kept her distance from the child.

****

That night, Yoninah was exhausted from their flight from the city and the days they had been trekking. When she lay down to sleep that night, she felt like she collapsed and slid into the bed she had as a small child. Even though it was actually straw on the floor of a donkey shed. She had a dream vision of her mother tucking her into bed, from when she was a child of no more than seven years. Her mother's touch, in her dream, transmuted into the gentle touch of the goddess—a luminous, all-encompassing presence – which provided her with a sense of safe shelter. Just like her mother mother's touch had, when she was little. When she woke up at dawn the next morning, she remembered this dream and was thankful for it.

****

Two more days of hard trekking followed, with two more nights sheltering in a donkey shed. The piles of stones indicating towns and shelter seemed to be spaced such that at the end of a long day's hike, one would appear. The townsfolk seemed happy, for a small price, to provide shelter and a modest dinner for the night.

****

Shelter in a Cave

The next day on the donkey trail, afternoon clouds started rolling in. A downpour followed, with claps of thunder and flashes of lightning. The travelers were getting soaked and their cloaks were little help. Nathan-El fared the best because he was sheltered under Laylah's cloak. At least the leather bags, with its stores of breads, grain, figs, and cheeses, stayed dry enough. They were hopeful when they passed a pile of stones but saw no shelter in sight.

"A cave! Off to the left!" Tahir shouted.

They scrambled up a rough slope to the mouth of the cave. Menelaus helped Gedalyah's grandma climb the slope. Her balance was not good. The goat, however, had no difficulty with the climb. Neither did the dog.

They made it to the cave and were grateful for the shelter it offered. The thunder and lightning quieted down, but the driving rain continued.

"We need to get out of these wet clothes," Gedalyah's grandmother said. "Let's see if anything is dry in the bags."

They changed into dry tunics and started a fire from twigs and branches near the cave that were mostly dry by virtue of a sharp overhang that sheltered them from the rain. They set up a camp of sorts.

The cave was spacious enough to accommodate seven sleeping mats. Tahir, with the goat and dog, had to sleep under the overhang, with a tarp rigged over them for extra protection.

Even though the rain continued, Menelaus picked up his bow and arrow and went hunting for rabbit or something for dinner.

The younger ones invented a game to keep them entertained for the remainder of the afternoon. Gedalyah unpacked his tablet of wax. He warmed the wax in the fire and when it was nicely softened, it could be used as a writing surface. He used his stylus to etch out the Ugaritic letters. Bat-El was intrigued and asked him to teach her what the letters meant.

Gedalyah spent the afternoon teaching her how to write the Ugaritic version of thirty cuneiform letters, each letter representing a sound. Bat-El was a quick study and seemed to enjoy learning the letters.

"It looks like a jumble of spears," Bat-El said of the Ugaritic cuneiform.

Bat-El drew pictures to represent the letters. She drew a sketch of an ox (the word for "ox" in Ugarit was "ah-lef") to represent the sound "ah." She drew a sketch of a house (the word for "house" in Ugarit was "bet") to represent the sound "beh." She drew a camel's hump (the word for "camel" in Ugarit was "gimmel") to represent the sound "geh." And so on, for another twenty or so letters.

Gedalyah had little patience for her artistic endeavors. Bat-El ignored his protests.

This amused the young people as the afternoon waned. Then Bat-El and Gedalyah got bored. They started writing insults to each other. Gedalyah wrote his in the Ugaritic cuneiform script: "You are a donkey!" Bat-El responded in her newly devised picture-script: "You are the donkey!"

"You are doing it wrong! That is not how the letters look!" Gedalyah said.

"Well, that's how they should look." Bat-El retorted.

"Nobody writes them that way," Gedalyah said.

"Well, someone should start writing them that way," Bat-El said. And they continued bickering.

Yoninah listened to this exchange. She found it both amusing and irritating. She was happy that the young people found a way to amuse themselves, but her patience was running thin. She could not take much more arguing. A pounding rain continued outside the shelter of the cave. Menelaus returned with three rabbits.

While they got a fire going, the makeshift family ate a dinner of roasted rabbit, flat bread and dates.

The fire was strategically located at the mouth of the cave, near the overhang. The cloud cover was dense, with a little light from the moon struggling through the clouds. The darkness would have been total except for the fire.

They kept it going as best they could by throwing fresh branches on it to nurse it along. The fire's light was comforting and also kept wild animals away.

With the comfort of food in their bellies, they spread out their sleeping mats, as well as their cloaks and blankets. The former had dried to some extent over the fire. The group went to sleep.

The baby nestled again between Bat-El and Laylah. Nathan-El ate bread soaked in goat milk, but this time with small pieces of rabbit meat added.

The baby had two teeth in his mouth, but that was all. Yoninah couldn't tell Nathan-El's age but estimated it at nine months. Whatever his age, he seemed to appreciate the meal. The baby even smiled for Bat-El as she covered him with a blanket and told him a little story – some nonsense about talking goats. He gurgled at the funny sounds she made, if not the actual story line, and fell asleep.

Yoninah herself did not fall asleep so easily. Menelaus was still awake, at the mouth of the cave. She went to sit with him.

They talked softly so as not to keep the others awake.

"We are getting close to Ur-Kataan," Menelaus said. "I am looking forward to seeing my son again. It's been a year since I saw him last. He is a good man. He will be happy to meet you and your brood."

"I am looking forward to an end to this trek," Yoninah leaned against Menelaus. "My feet hurt. My skin is burnt from the sun. My daughter Bat-El is picking fights with Gedalyah. Although Tahir has been a good companion. And Laylah clearly enjoys his company."

She was silent for a moment

"The new baby is finding his way into the hearts of the young people," Yoninah said. "You are a good man, for having rescued him from the burning city."

When they fell silent, she could smell his body and she could hear his breathing. She also listened to the sound of the rain on the rocky roof overhead. She felt comforted next to

Menelaus. She was even comforted somehow by the young people and their familiar bickering.

At a time when everything else that was familiar had been taken from her, she was deeply grateful for Menelaus' company and that of the quarrelsome young people. She went back inside and held those thoughts as she fell into a deep sleep.

By the next morning, the storm had cleared. They packed up their belongings and headed out again. Unfortunately, the donkey trail was partly washed away. A mudslide had blocked their path. They had to stop long enough to throw chunks of mud and rocks off the trail before they could continue on the path.

The girls and Gedalyah complained of their hands and feet getting muddy.

"Get used to it, princesses." He thought this was amusing, but no one else did.

****

Hot Springs, Last Day on the Donkey Trail

The following day, they hiked a distance and suddenly smelled the odor of rotten eggs.

"Is this the gateway to the underworld? Is that why it smells funny?" Bat-El asked.

"It's a hot spring, NOT the gateway to the underworld," Menelaus said. "There are hot springs scattered throughout these mountains."

The group of them went down a short distance to investigate. A narrow trail led through the brush, to a spring of hot water gushing forth from a crevice in the rocks. The water cascaded down into a rocky pool. Steam rose in the morning air. Clearly, the water was hot. And smelling of sulfur, as Bat-El had noted.

"We can go into the water, if you like," Menelaus said. "The pool is warm. But do not put your hand in the water coming directly from the crevice in the rock. That water is scalding hot. You would get a good burn that way."

"A good soak in a hot spring works wonders for sore muscles," Menelaus added.

By this point, Menelaus and Tahir took off their muddy tunics, leaving them naked except for their loincloths. They waded into the water. Gedalyah, never the most adventurous of men, did the same. There was a natural staircase going down as a formation of stones. There were thankfully smooth stones under their feet as well.

Menelaus called out from the pool. "Come on in! The water is fine."

The womenfolk were at a loss. They were not about to take off their tunics for this adventure.

"Go on in, youngsters," Gedalyah's grandmother said. "Get your clothes wet. They would benefit from a wash anyway. I'll fetch dry clothes from our packs on the trail above. You can change after your soak."

Yoninah and the girls waded into the water. The warmth of the water felt good, Yoninah thought. She closed her eyes for a moment. She opened her eyes again when she felt a tap on her shoulder.

Bat-El was holding the baby.

"Will you hold him? I want to get good and wet," Bat-El said.

Yoninah took the baby, who was fascinated by all the splashing and soaking going on around him. The child began to splash as well. He seemed perfectly comfortable in this new environment. His evident enjoyment of the water made Yoninah smile.

Yoninah felt her cold heart give way just a smidgeon. Maybe she could find a way to bond to this small person. She held him while he splashed madly in the water. She dipped him a short distance into the water, which he tolerated well. He held onto to her arm with a death grip, however. He clearly was not going to let go of her, no matter what.

Grandmother returned from her foray through their packs on the trail and found several clean, dry tunics in there. Tahir had evidently packed extra clothing. He was vain about his clothing. But he agreed to let the women folk use his clean tunics as they chose.

When they finished their bathing interlude, the men put back on their somewhat dirty tunics over their thoroughly wet loincloths. They left the women alone, to let them take off their wet clothes and change into fresh dry ones.

And the entourage, newly refreshed by the healing waters of the hot springs, continued their trip along the donkey trail. By late afternoon, another pile of stones appeared off to the side of the road.

"That is Ur-Kataan! Its name means small town. And it is indeed small," Menelaus said.

The group assembled at the overlook. They saw below them the river they had been following throughout. At this point, the river cut through a generous valley, with enough acreage for grains and for vines. Enough grasses to feed cows and goats and sheep.

The walls of the little town below looked sturdy enough and well-built enough to hold up through natural hazards such as earthquakes and storms. Maybe not invaders. But then again, what invader sought a small town this distance inland and so far from the trade routes?

The group of seven people—plus baby, goat, and dog-- admired the view in silence for a few minutes. Yoninah felt a lessening of the dread she had carried with her since leaving her home, since she had seen the city burn. After being homeless and a wanderer on the land, she felt a stirring of hope.

"I think we can make a home here." Yoninah said.

She did not know if she could pick up the pieces of her craft or if she could continue working as a healer. She did not know if her children would be happy in this little town. She did not know if Menelaus would find work here, or Tahir for that matter. She did not know if their newly adopted child would thrive in their care.

"We are all in the hands of the gods. Whatever they plan for us, we must accept," Yoninah said.

And, with that, they started walking down into the valley below, to the little town awaiting them.

PART 5: ON THE SEA

An Ancient Sailor's Prayer

"O great and mighty Baal – Rider of the Clouds, Master of the Winds, he who slew the great sea serpent Lotan –send us gentle winds to fill our sails and gentle waves to mark our passage. Protect us from raging storms. Keep the great sea monsters far from us. And guide us safely to our destination."

--Adapted from Baal's battle with Lotan. See Coogan 2012

CHAPTER 33: ON THE SEA: THUT-MOSES AND THE SHEKELESH

As the camp of refugees prepared for their trek along the highway and into the mountains… Thut-Moses had been taken prisoner by the seaborne attackers.

When Thut-Moses had put down his weapon and had raised his hands in surrender, he had been taken captive by the enemy and led away to their ships.

****

As he and his captors made their way to their ships, Thut-Moses saw them loot houses for whatever grain, wine, or gold they could find. He and a whole line of captives, all tied together, were loaded onto a black-flagged ship which had been anchored a short distance from shore.

A plank had been lowered. The returning soldiers mounted the plank and gained the ship. So did the captives.

The foreign sailors and crew pointed at him as he boarded. He assumed they had never seen an overly tall Nubian before. Beardless, to boot. Given his status as a eunuch, he was unable to grow a beard.

As the ships pulled out of the harbor, he saw thick smoke rise above the city. The enemy had torched the city. He thought, "I hope the king and David are safe." He knew that the wives and children were safe. They had left two weeks earlier. For this, he was grateful. He thought, "The King and his bard should be on their way to join them in their 'summer retreat'."

His captors spoke a godforsaken language. Their helmets had horns on them. Their hair was light-colored, their eyes blue; their skin a shade lighter than that of the Canaanites.

Thut-Moses thought, "I am truly a captive," As prisoners, the men taken from Ugarit were tied by shackles to the oars during the day. At night, the ship would head towards shore and drop anchor. The men would be allowed to go ashore and set up rough camps on the sand with guards set as sentries, to ensure that no one tried to escape.

Thut-Moses joined the oarsmen in the galley. It was hard work. He was not as strong as some of the other men. As a scribe, he had had no reason to build up muscles. But he built up his muscles in the days to follow. He ate the gruel that passed for nourishment; drank the beer they were given. He thought, "They are feeding us enough to keep our strength up, no more."

****

In the next few days, he settled into the rhythm of life as an oarsman on a boat commanded by foreign pirates and of Mycenean workmanship. Thut-Moses saw their trajectory: to follow the shoreline south, to the other rich seaports that lined the eastern margin of the Great Sea.

****

In the days to come, Thut-Moses watched as the sea raiders attacked two other towns along the coast. He grew numb to the level of destruction they left behind. Even though he had read the annals, the prayers, and he knew from a scholarly perspective that cities get burnt and people get killed, even though he had experienced the looting and burning of Ugarit, the harsh reality of it was a shock.

When a likely town was sighted, the ships would come close to the land, with the goal either of dropping anchor near the beach or of landing on the sand itself. The ships were shallow draught and perfectly suited for a smooth approach to the beach.. Thut-Moses would watch the warriors –with their long swords and shields—disembark, along with the men assigned to carry back the booty. The rowers would then be waiting for the booty and the warriors to make their way back from the pillaging and swordplay. The warriors, on their return, were invariably sporting patches of dried blood on their clothes. Not their own blood, that of their victims.

The town they had pillaged would be burning. The ship's crew could even hear the wails of women mourning the loss of husbands and of children. Smoke from the fires would drift out to sea.

The oarsmen would then power their exodus, their return to the waves of the Great Sea. And, with luck, sea winds would fill the sail and the men at the oars could rest for a bit. As they travelled to their next destination—their next target—another seaport on the coast, another source of grain and booty.

At sunset, the men would make camp on the shore. With luck, a fire would be started. It offered scant comfort, however. They would have a meal of gruel, cheese, and beer.

On the sixth night, as the men sat around the fire and ate their evening meal, they watched as lightning flickered on the horizon. The stars were brilliant against the sky, a half moon offering some light. A fellow oarsman engaged Thut-Moses in conversation. Thut-Moses was relieved to find a fellow fugitive from Ugarit. The Ugarit man had been on a Cypriot vessel making landfall in Miletos when it was overtaken by the sea raiders.

"Our captors are called 'Shekelesh.', the man said. They are one of several tribes in confederation. Other ships in the convoy are manned by a tribe called Peleset."

"Shekelesh?" Thut-Moses sounded out the word carefully. "I have heard that name before, from a clay tablet I saw…"

"The Shekelesh might be refugees from the north – from the Black Sea or even further. I understand they are fleeing a great drought and crop failures. Other tribes are refugees from Mycenae and elsewhere in the Aegean. Often drafted into the sea raider fleet after their own towns had been leveled and they were left with few other options."

That night, as Thut-Moses made up his crude bed of palm fronds on the sand, he briefly puzzled over the movements of people from distant lands and the forces that would drive people to leave their homes. He was too tired to give it much thought. As he listened to the sounds of night birds cawing and of waves slapping against the shore, he fell asleep.

He had a dream. He was sleeping in a proper bed, with blankets and soft pillows. He had a proper meal for breakfast: cakes and cheeses and figs. In the morning, he woke up to a rough sleeping mat and a bowl of gruel for breakfast.

During his days at the oars, he kept a vision of returning to life in a palace in the front of his mind: surrounded not only by food and furniture but also by scrolls and tablets. It kept him from going mad as he kept pace with the other oarsmen.

****

Thut-Moses and the Raging Sea

After four weeks of hard travel, weeks of pulling on the oars to the beat of drums, Thut-Moses' shoulders and back ached. He was not used to hard physical labor, not used to scant food.

Thut-Moses was also not used to seatmates from the lower reaches of society. They cursed a great deal. He understood their curses, he understood their language. Most of them were taken from other Canaanite cities and spoke a dialect he could understand. At sunset, they would moor the ships in shallow waters, drop the gangplank, and head to the sandy beaches. With guards keeping them under observation, to keep them from escaping into the nearby woods.

They spent their nights sleeping with scant comfort on the sand.. The sounds of night birds, the growls of wild animals that hunt at night kept Thut-Moses awake at first. He found some comfort in watching the splendor of the sunsets over the western sea; the blazing oranges and yellows as the sun sank into the darkening sea.

The Shekelesh had taken more captives from the towns they attacked. They were brought back to the ship, in ropes linked to one another.

The new arrivals were young men, by and large. The work was hard. Thut-Moses suspected that their overlords would work them to death without any compunction. The best hope for himself and the other captives would be if they were sold and got off the galley. Maybe they would find less-dangerous work on dry land.

One ship in the convoy had women and children on it. They were apparently moving entire families. The families slept on board ship, as they were anchored offshore. He caught an occasional glimpse of the women and children. The women were tall like the men. Buxom, with yellow hair. The children pointed at him. They had never seen a black man before, he guessed. He did not smile at them. He did not want to continue the interaction.

These people were wiry and strong. They spoke a language he could make no inroads with, nothing he had ever heard before.

On the fortieth day, while they were crossing the open sea, a storm blew up. The ship rocked in the massive waves, with water splashing onto her decks. A gust of wind blew so hard, it ripped out the sail from its rigging. The sailors clearly got scared.

They signaled for Thut-Moses to come on the foredeck and make an incantation to the gods of the sea, in case he had special magic to tame the storm. They released him from the chains that bound his ankle to the wooden bench in the galley.

Thut-Moses made it to the foredeck, although the ship was unsteady and he almost fell. In the driving rain, he raised his right arm to the sky and got soaked for his efforts. He clutched the rail with his left hand to keep from being swept overboard. He recited a prayer his father had taught him, in his native Nubian, with some amendments.

"Oh mighty gods, listen to the prayer of your humble servant. Let these godforsaken foreigners go to a watery death. Then let the anger of the sea god be assuaged. Let the storm remit. Let the waves become gentle once more. Let me and my fellows get off these hell hole of a ship and see the next morning."

He recited this in a loud voice, with a rhythmic beat, in imitation of the priestly prayers he had heard in Egypt and in Ugarit. It was an impressive performance: an unnaturally tall man with a handsome face and ebony skin, holding court with the gods in the midst of a tempest.

The rains abated. The winds grew less brutal. The sails had been shredded by the winds. The sailors nodded their approbation for his magical touch. And escorted him back down to the hold. Where he rejoined his fellow oarsmen as they made for the safety of a nearby beach.

That evening, when they set up a crude camp on the sandy beach, Thut-Moses was given ample room. The other oarsmen were a bit in awe of him. Their captors gave them the usual dinner of hard bread, even harder cheese, and dried dates. They gave Thut-Moses an extra piece of bread and an unexpected cup of red wine. He thought: "None of them speak Nubian. They do not know that I cursed them. Which curse apparently did not take hold. The godforsaken foreigners are still alive. But so is the crew, so that is a blessing."

They stayed camped on the beach for an extra day, to gain time to repair the sails. And to stock up on fresh water and whatever livestock they could steal from the surrounding villages. They roasted four sheep they had stolen and slaughtered and even had a repast of meat on their second night on the beach. Then set out again, heading further south, on the open waters of the sea.

****

Thut-Moses Arrives in Tyre

After eight weeks onboard the foreign ship, after ravaging a score of seaports along the eastern shores of the Great Sea, Thut-Moses and his shipmates reached the island of Tyre. They could see several other ships crowded into the harbor. Ships belonging to Tyre herself, as well as ships from her sister cities, Byblos and Sidon.

Their black-flagged ship made anchor and dropped a plank, allowing access to the shallow water and to the beach. The Shekelesh as well as their captives all splashed to shore.

As Thut-Moses and his fellow oarsmen made their way ashore, he thought: "Well, this is different. No taking of a beach, no storming of city gates."

Gulls circled above. The sea winds blew, and with them the scent of salt in the air.

Tyre loomed above them, on the high point of this little island. Like Ugarit, it had a tower with a fire burning throughout the night, to guide ships at sea. It too had brothels and inns. The men just offloaded from their ship joined the throng of people in the harbor-- mostly native Tyrians in their customary tunics and headbands.

Somehow Tyre had become a sanctuary, where the sea raiders stopped to rest and to pick up provisions. Thut-Moses could only guess that Tyre and the Shekelesh or Peleset – whichever tribes were there--had struck a treaty: Tyre would sell them food and beer and other necessities. In exchange, they would leave her standing. They would neither loot nor burn her to the ground.

His heart lightened at this thought. Perhaps Tyre would be a good refuge for him as well. If he could convince or convey to the slaver who would buy him that he had connections in the palace…if he could recall his Tyrian contact's name, perhaps he could obtain sanctuary in the court as a scribe and leave behind this godforsaken life as an oarsman on an enemy ship….

Their captors wasted no time in conveying their cargo to the slave market. It was only a short distance from the harbor. Their ship's captain himself led the men—their hands tied in ropes—to a paved square. They were lined up on an elevated stage. The buyers of slaves would look them over. Grading them on youth, on how strong they looked. How much they would bring in from a would-be client who needed a strong man to carry cargo or to harvest the grain or to drive the donkeys and oxen that fueled the grain press.

One man after another was auctioned off. Thut Muses was left standing, with two other who were also deemed too slender or too effete to count. Someone made a bid for him.He Thut-Moses was asked to speak. They wanted to make sure he had a voice.

"I am a scribe, Take me to Hadid, advisor to your king. He will pay good money for me!" Thut-Moses said in a clear voice, with the accent of Ugarit.

The slave traders understood the concept of money. One of their number, a grizzled, rough-looking man, paid quickly for Thut-Moses. By then, the bidding was not that brisk.

"My name is Nachash," the grizzled man smiled, revealing a row of rotten teeth. His eyes glittered with a warning. "For your sake, I hope you are a valuable scribe. Otherwise, you are too scrawny to be of much use."

Thut-Moses felt a small measure of relief as Nachash brought him to a bathhouse where he could clean up. Thut-Moses received a clean tunic. His hair was still wild and untrimmed. But at least his beard had not grown. The slave trader fed him a decent meal and gave him a crude bed to sleep on that night.

In the morning, Nachash took him to the palace. Thut-Moses' arms were again in ropes. At the gate to the palace, the slave trader told Thut-Moses to repeat what he had told him at the harbor. "I am a scribe. Take me to Hadid."" The guard at the gate turned them over to another man. The second man took them to the palace quarters occupied by Hadid.

The emissary was seated at a handsome table, with the morning light slanting in from a generous slit of a window. He looked up at the interruption. At first, he looked confused. Then he said, "By the gods, this is Thut-Moses, the scribe from Ugarit! You look terrible! What have they done to you?"

The guard had kept hold of Thut-Moses' arm. He let go of the arm. Nachash, behind him, looked delighted. He became effusive: "Your fine honor, we took this man from the battlements of Ugarit. He is a captive. He says he knows you…"

"Of course he knows me! You fool, unhand him! Let him sit with me and tell me his story."

The slave trader looked reluctant to leave, given that no money had crossed his palm. The emissary said: "Go, go! I will send you whatever price is required! Come back later today. But leave the man here. I need to talk to him…."

And Thut-Moses gratefully took a seat. His host offered him red wine and cheese and figs. Purveyed on a small table, for his enjoyment. He was famished and took it gratefully.

Thut-Moses told Hadid about what had transpired, that last day in Ugarit. "I was at the battlements with bow and arrow and did what I could. The enemy far outnumbered us and they were heavily armed. I surrendered and they took me and fellow captives onto their ship. And put us to work as oarsmen.".

He paused briefly, "I wasn't very good at the oars. I am too tall."

Hadid chuckled at Thut-Moses' admission. "Now that's a waste of a fine mind," Hadid said.

"When we got to Tyre, I remembered your kind words, at that banquet in Ugarit. You said, 'If ever you need refuge, come to Tyre.'"

His host said, "Yes, I meant it. We can use a skilled scribe such as yourself. Let us have another cup of wine to celebrate your new position!" Hadid gestured to the servants, who quickly reappeared with another carafe.

"And what happened to the King and the Queen that you became friends with? A lovely lady, Queen Donotiya. She told me about your literary encounters, as she called them. "

"They should be safe in their mountain retreat by now." Thut-Moses savored the wine, an excellent vintage. The Queen left a week or two before the attack. The King left the day of the attack. He took a passageway in the lower level, in between the granaries, that would take him to outside the city walls.

Where horses and ox-carts would have awaited. As far as I know, they are all safe.

"And the handsome musician? The one who sang the story of Aquat?" Hadid smiled at the memory of the banquet's entertainment.

"He kept the King company, as he fled through the hidden passage. He too should be safe."

"And the city itself?"

"The city is gone. Pillaged and torched. Nothing left standing." Thut-Moses paused in his retelling of the events of that day.

"These Shekelesh or Peleset, whoever they are, they are efficient at attacking and pillaging," Thut-Moses continued. "I will give them that. Although they seem to be giving Tyre a wide berth…. I assume you have a peace treaty with them? I hope you do. I would indeed like to stay here, in the court of Tyre. "

And so it was arranged: Thut-Moses assumed a position as a scribe in the Tyrian court. Hadid himself took him under his wing, for which he was grateful. He got to wear fine clothes again. He got to bathe regularly and to have his hair trimmed. He got fine foods again. And he got to scribe again, reading and replying to letters from what was left of the Great Sea trading ports.

PART 6: SIX YEARS LATER

Life is fleeting…no one has returned form the hereafter, to tell us of their lot, to set our hearts at ease. So rejoice your heart! Absence of care is good for you; follow your heart as long as you live. Put myrrh on your head, dress yourself in fine linen, anoint yourself with fine oils. Let your belly be full... Pay heed to the little one that holds on to your hand. Let your spouse delight in your bosom. For this is the task of mankind!

Adapted from the "Song of the Harper," from Egypt, circa 2000 BC (see Coogan, 2013); and from the *Alewife's Tale*, (Epic of Gilgamesh)

Chapter 34: UR-KATAAN, SIX YEARS AFTER THE FALL OF UGARIT

"Grandmother, tell me a story!" said the little girl.

"Five years old and so precocious," thought the grandmother. "So good with words, so eager for stories at night."

The grandmother couldn't resist the child, who looked up at her with pleading hazel eyes beneath brown hair.

The grandmother sat down on the bed beside the girl. "What story do you want?"

"How about the one about the house you grew up in?" said the girl. "And about the languages you heard people talk and the monkeys you saw in the street?"

"I will tell you a story about the house I grew up in, and the people and monkeys in the street." Yoninah made the story take a while. She tried to bore the child into sleep by describing in detail the sailors in the street and their clothing and the languages they spoke. She told her granddaughter about the monkey on the street corner, chittering away, and the little red hat the monkey wore.

Shoshana was finally getting sleepy. Yoninah felt pleased after a long day of washing clothes in the river and drying them on the rocks, followed by Laylah helping to plant a herb garden for the year. The garden was planted with seeds for Valerian, so carefully saved from last year. Menelaus had cleared the garden for the house that they shared with Laylah and her family.

Tahir came in the room. Just like a man, to interrupt the child's bedtime, Yoninah thought ruefully to herself.

"So there's my little Princess. Let me have a kiss, short stuff." Tahir said. The little girl obliged, giving him a kiss and a hug.

But now her granddaughter was awake again. Tahir had to tell her a story this time because Yoninah was too tired. He told her a silly story about a talking donkey, who was complaining bitterly of how hungry he was. Tahir was good at imitating voices, including imaginary donkey voices. The little girl finally grabbed her doll, turned on her side, snuggled into her blanket and fell asleep.

Laylah had quietly joined them by that point. She had been busy weaving cloth in the last light of day. The three of them went to the rooftop veranda. An evening breeze blew across the roof. The moon was almost full and provided ample light. Potted plants added to the atmosphere, as well as jars for collecting rainwater. They sat on stools and shared a flask of wine watered down with water. An excellent vintage, from this year's first harvest. Menelaus had given them the flask.

"Any more trips this month?" asked Laylah. Tahir was always going off with the donkey. He would load it up with grain and wine and trade in surrounding villages for food, spices, herbs, or shekels. He also brought back tunics made of fine linen for festival days. These festivals were not as numerous or as grand as the ones held at the Temple of Baal in Ugarit but still required linen tunics at the temple in the town.

"Maybe one more trip this month, and two more trips next month. It will be hot by then. I might stay here and take it easy in the shade of the house. Maybe help out in the vineyards. Help with the first harvest in late summer." he said.

"I miss the streets of Ugarit. But this is a good life too. Different, but good," Laylah stifled a yawn.

Yoninah looked at the young couple and tried to hide a smile. Laylah had told her mother that she had missed her monthly flow. Laylah hadn't told Tahir yet, she said, but she hoped it was a boy this time.

"He could teach a boy the fine arts of trade and how to press grapes into wine. And how to fight with a lance. Tahir would enjoy that." Laylah had told her mother.

CHAPTER 39: MENELAUS

Menelaus was now in his fifties. He missed the taverns in Ugarit and drinking beers with the sailors. But he enjoyed working in the vineyards, alongside his son. He also enjoyed the conversations with his seven-year-old grandson and his five-year-old granddaughter. He considered them both exceptionally bright and handsome.

Menelaus told them stories from his own childhood; stories his grandmother had told him. His grandmother was from Crete and knew the old stories, from before the Mycenaeans took over the island.

Their favorite story was about the boy with wings.

"Dedalus was a clever man who could build wondrous things. He worked for the King of Crete. making fine bows for archers and beautifully crafted chairs. Dedalus wanted to go to Egypt, to see the wonderful things they made there. The king did not want him to leave." Menelaus acted out both parts for his grandchildren.

"So Dedalus fashioned wings for himself and his young son – wings of bird feathers fixed to a wooden frame with wax. And he and his son slipped away, so the king wouldn't know. They went to a high cliff overlooking the sea. Dedalus put the wings over his shoulders and fixed them to his son's shoulders as well. And then they leapt off. The wind caught their wings and they flew! Dedalus said to his son: 'Don't fly too high, that's the only thing. The sun will melt the wax!' But the boy of course paid no mind. He got so excited; he flew higher and higher. The wax melted. The feathers fell off. He fell into the sea."

The little girl, who always listened closely, would look sad at this part. "He fell? Are you sure he fell?"

"Yes, I am sure he fell." Menelaus would pause for a moment. "The moral of this story? Listen to your father! Or your grandfather, for that matter."

Menelaus finished the story and tucked the children into bed.

****

He had been worried about Yoninah when they fled from Ugarit. He had been afraid she would fall into another deep sorrow, like the experience she described after the deaths of her captain and her newborn baby. But she had come through the trek and the transition to their new lives in Ur-Kataan. She had started smiling again and teasing him and the children. She had taken their newly-adopted son into her heart. And seemed to look at the boy with adoration even if he were up to mischief. It filled his own heart; to see the pleasure she took in the boy..

****

Yoninah

Yoninah was older as well, with a few gray hairs sprinkled in her black curls. Her practice as a healer was thriving. Patients were different in this little village. No more sailors needing amulets to protect them on sea voyages. But the townspeople from Ur-Kataan still suffered from heartbreak, infertility, or childbirth. They still needed sleep draughts and medicine for pain or coughs.

She enjoyed conversations with her patients. She felt welcome in their little community. They hadn't had a healer for decades. People sought her out from the neighboring villages as well.

She grew as many herbs she could. Tahir would buy opium and other exotic medical plants from traders on the road to Hamath or from traders coming from the Tigris-Euphrates.

****

It had taken Yoninah taken some time to take joy in her new son. They had named him "Nathan-El, ". meaning "gift from god." At first, Bat-El and Laylah watched him. After a month or so, Yoninah started taking care of him. She would put him to bed and rub his back as he fell asleep. She was thrilled that he relaxed under her hand. She started looking forward to this nightly ritual. She felt the chill in her heart melt. She grew to love him. "The human heart is resilient," Yoninah thought to herself.

She enjoyed watching Nathan-El grow. He was an affectionate child with an easy-going nature despite his rough start in life. He liked to help Menelaus at the vineyards. It was debatable how much help he was. He liked going on trips with

Uncle Tahir, who let him lead the donkey as they went on short trips to nearby villages. He was learning to count shekels.

Life in Ur-kataan

Yoninah still spoke to her dead relatives. She had constructed small shrines in a room of their house. One was for her mother; another for the captain; and the third for her stillborn son. She visited the shrines on the day of the new moon. She kept her mother up to date on the patients she had seen and how her granddaughters were doing. She told the captain how the girls were all grown up and how Ur-Kataan had been good for them. She told the baby that she still missed him. That she was so sorry she never watched him grow up. And she told him about Nathan-El, his brother of sorts.

At times, Yoninah missed the sights and sounds of Ugarit. She still had vivid dreams of walking down Palace Street, watching the slave girls running past, their colorful skirts flying as they ran. Yoninah dreamed of handsome young sailors, with their strong legs on display, underneath their short tunics. In her dreams, the voice of the seller of execration stones called out his curses. The prostitutes with their kohl-lined eyes and henna-enhanced hair and red color on their lips also called out to passersby. The little monkey appeared with its hand extended.

In her dream, Yoninah would be carrying her medicinal plants – cannabis, valerian root, poppy seed —and trying to find her house. But the streets were jumbled. She was not able to find her house, which seemed to keep getting further away, the more she walked. Suddenly she was floating a short distance above the street. At this point, she would wake up and realize it was a dream.

****

In Ur-Kataan, stray travelers brought reports of cities being destroyed along the coast. Yoninah and Menelaus heard tales of widespread destruction with scores of cities being leveled and burnt.

Their days in this small village devolved into a simpler lifestyle. The villages survived. But the cosmopolitan seaports were gone.

The village grew its own food. Fine linens from Egypt were a thing of the past, as were luxuries such as perfume, hair fillets, and kohl. Figs and dates were still available, sourced from local orchards. Goats provided milk for cheese, and an occasional offering of newborn kid goats. Yoninah and the girls had plenty of wool on hand, but they had to do their own weaving. Nonetheless, she woke up every morning, grateful to be alive.

****

Full Moon Ceremony

The family made a custom of going on an occasional pilgrimage to the hot springs. Tahir and Menelaus would accompany them, serving as armed escorts along the donkey trail. The roads were not entirely secure.

The family would go on the day of the full moon because it was an auspicious day to visit. They would eat a noontime meal at home and then start their hike. They would get there by mid-afternoon and then visit the warm waters. After an evening meal, they would return to the pool. Under the bright light of the moon, they would immerse themselves again in the healing waters and offer prayers to the gods. They thanked them for their good fortune in surviving the fall of Ugarit and then asked for their further protection.

Nathan-El had grown up with these pilgrimages. He took them as a matter of course. He continued to enjoy bouncing in the hot springs, even at age seven.

When she could, Bat-El would come to the hot springs. She still enjoyed playing with Nathan-El. She was busy with the little school for scribes that she and her betrothed, Gedalyah, had started in Ur-Kataan.

Laylah and Tahir still came to the hot spring. Their daughter demanded as much.

Yoninah and Menelaus enjoyed their pilgrimages to the hot springs as much as the younger people did. Menelaus enjoyed the healing waters. The hot water soothed his aches and pains. Yoninah found the pilgrimage soothing not only for her tired muscles but also for her soul. Under the magical light of the full moon, she felt that she was connecting with larger forces in the universe--with the gods--for whom the fortunes of individuals were of minor concern. All sorts of mayhem occurred on the human level and the universe still went on, in its destined and mysterious fashion. For some reason, she found this comforting. Her mission was to make the best life she could for herself and her loved ones. Which was enough. And if she asked for occasional help from the gods, perhaps they would listen.

PART 7: SIX YEARS LATER: A SCRIBE IN EGYPT

It is better to be a scribe than to be a rich man who builds a fine house. A rich man dies; his corpse is dust. Doors and mansions fall. His name is forgotten. But a scribe…. His work lives on, his name lives on, in the scrolls that he writes. For generations to come, people repeat his words and recite his name.

--Adapted from "In Praise of Scribes," Egypt circa 1300 BC. See Coogan 2013.

Chapter 35: THUT-MOSES IN EGYPT

Six years later, in Egypt… Thut-Moses was a newly arrived scribe in the court of Ramses III.

Pharoah requested his attendance at an interview in the throne room.

As Thut-Moses was escorted from his new quarters in the palace and across the grand plaza, he passed two statues carved out of stone. Each stood at a height equal to his own. They were painted in bright colors. Standing guard, one on each side of the grand doors that led into the royal quarters. He recognized one figure as Horus with the head of a hawk. The other figure was that of Sekhmet, with the head of a lioness.

"I see that Horus and Sekhmet are standing guard on the Pharaoh," Thut-Moses said to his escort. He was happy enough to see them there. He would much rather have the fierce god and goddess fighting on the Pharoah's side than otherwise.

As he appeared before Pharoah, Thut-Moses hoped his appearance looked worthy of this elegant court. He wore the full-length white robes of the Egyptian court, with a chain around his neck that displayed the figure of Isis. The amulet was the same one the healer in Ugarit had given him years before. Thut-Moses knew he made a striking figure, with his dark skin and height, against the red walls of the throne room and the colorful frescoes showing scenes along the Nile.

Thut-Moses made the requisite bow before Pharaoh. Ramses III was himself a tall man, with chiseled features and a majestic beak-shaped nose. He sat on a throne that gleamed with gold fixtures. A councilor stood next to the throne: a tall man with sharp eyes and a face creased by signs of age.

"We know you are from Ugarit," Pharaoh waved his hand with an air of command. "Tell us about the last days of the city, how you came to be a scribe in Tyre and now in Egypt."

"I was a scribe to Ammurabi , King of Ugarit, for fifteen years," Thut-Moses said." "The King was pleased with my work and promoted me to his aide as well. In the year of the attack on the sun – if his majesty recalls, this was six years ago, in late summer—the city was attacked." The Pharoah nodded as if confirming the solar event.

"By early summer of that year, the city was lacking an army and a navy. The Hittites—to whom we were vassals, as the

Pharoah knows-- had already requisitioned both our fleet and our soldiers. They were under attack themselves." Pharaoh made a face at the mention of the Hittites.

"The attack on Ugarit came early one morning, in late summer. We had forewarnings: towns had been pillaged and burnt a short distance from Ugarit. We advised the population to prepare for evacuation. So, when enemy ships were spotted approaching our beach early the next day, the warnings went out and the city folk fled through the streets." Thut-Moses took a steadying breath before continuing his tale.

"King Ammurabi had his captain of the Guards organize what troops we had. We were greatly outnumbered by the sea raiders. They were well-armed, with fierce swords and shields."

"I am handy with bow and arrow," Thut-Moses said with modesty. "I was there, at the main gate of the palace wall, when they cut down the doors with massive bronze axes. The enemy breached the wall. After further fighting in the streets, I surrendered. They tied my hands together and marched me and several other men back to their ships."

"The foreigners looted and emptied the houses, palace, and temple. They set the city on fire as they left."

"What became of the king and his family?" Pharoah asked.

"They escaped through an underground passage and got to safety in their mountain retreat. Ammurabi sent me word while I was in Tyre. He reported that they are well. Although the wives are upset that they do not get any cosmetics or incense or perfumes anymore." Thut-Moses shared this information with a smile, which the councilor at least appreciated. Pharoah was still focused on serious matters

"Tell us about the people who captured you." Pharoah said.

"Yes, your Majesty," said Thut-Moses, with a deferential nod of his head. "They called themselves the 'Shekelesh' and they live on their ships. They speak a guttural language that is harsh on the ears. They are very tall, and they wear strange helmets and kilts. Their hair is light-colored and their skin is burnt from the sun." Pharaoh raised his eyebrows at the description.

"The men from Ugarit, we were prisoners on their ship; tied up by shackles to the oars. It was a hard life. I was an oarsman on their ship for all of eight weeks, while they continued down the eastern coast of the Great Sea, pillaging and burning one seaport after another."

"Then you came to Tyre, I take it?" asked Pharaoh.

"Yes, your eminence. We got to the city of Tyre. As my master knows, it is one of three sister-cites – Byblos and Sidon being the other two. These marauders were allies with the three cities... They did not loot them or set them on fire. The King of Tyre needed a skilled scribe. The Shekelesh sold me to him."

"The people in Tyre speak a language closely related to Ugarit. I could understand them. I could scribe for them." Thut-Moses made a writing gesture with his right hand.

"Over the next year or two, the merchants of Tyre were building up the trade routes, replacing the traffic that had gone through Ugarit. They were sending ships again to Egypt, Cyprus, and the Aegean. I shared with the city merchants what I knew about trade. They were grateful for what information I could provide."

The councilor nodded at Thut-Moses, indicating his appreciation for Thut-Moses' skill in trade matters.

"I also introduced to the court in Tyre a new way to scribe. I taught them a simplified version of the Ugaritic script. This new script is called the 'Alef-Bet,' your Majesty. Your scribes may have seen it in use, in their contacts with Tyre and the other two cities."

Thut-Moses saw the councilor again nod sagely, this time at his mention of a new script. Pharoah was unimpressed.

"I was in Tyre for six years. Then your majesty inquired if the King of Tyre had a scribe who could understand Egyptian. I was trained in Egypt and learnt hieratics as a boy. I came to the court in Thebes. This for me was a cause for joy. "

"We know these marauders," Pharoah said. "They came to Egypt when Merneptah was Pharaoh, thirty years ago. We called them the Sea Peoples. We fought with them and drove them away. These marauders, the Sea Peoples, are they coming again to Egypt? "

"Yes, my liege," Thut-Moses bowed his head. "The Sea Peoples, as you call them, are coming to Egypt. They seek the rich harvests of grain provided by the bounty of the Nile and the gold of Egypt."

"Can you predict how they will attack?" asked the councilor.

"They will try to enter the Nile at the Delta. Their goal would be to do this unobserved, probably by approaching the shores of Avaris or another city on the Nile and launching a rapid sortie. That is how they maneuvered along the coast of Canaan, your honor. They brought their low-draught ships ashore and landed on the beach; quickly unloading their warriors and attacking the city before alarms were sounded."

"And how do we counter this?" asked the councilor.

"Their ships may not be able to operate like this in the Delta, your honor. There are no beaches to land on, for a start. The channels are narrow and marshy in the Delta. The shores are covered by reeds. That would impede their progress. His Majesty could set up an ambush, catch them while they are still at anchor. before they can advance any distance into the Delta. Before they can off-load their warriors."

"Do you have any other advice for the court?" asked Pharaoh.

"Yes. There is something else in Egypt's favor, your majesty," answered Thut-Moses." The Sea Peoples have been at war for over six years now. Their forces are most likely depleted, along with their strength and spirits."

"Is there anything else we should know? Any other invaders coming this way?" asked the councilor.

"There is also a land-based force, my lord. The forces that attacked the Hittite capital traveled on land. They had oxen carrying women and children. I'm not sure if they are the same tribes as in the seaborne force. But they are also a threat. They too would be seeking the wealth of Egypt. They would approach across Sinai, my lord. If they attack, it would be at that border."

The councilor nodded at Thut-Moses, indicating his appreciation for the advice he was giving.

"We will position lookouts and spies at both the mouth of the Delta and across the border with Sinai," said the Pharoah with hardness to his voice.

Thut-Moses bowed before the Pharoah. "I hope my lord Pharoah and his court have found this information useful."

"Yes, it has been useful," said the Pharoah, waving a jeweled hand. "You may go."

Thut-Moses did another graceful bow. He did the ritual six steps back and bowed again. He saw the councilor smile at him as he left.

****

The Tale of "Two Brothers"

Thut-Moses returned to his apartment in the grand palace of the Pharaoh. He appreciated that it had a spacious balcony through which he could see the fountains, pools, and gardens of the palace courtyard. He made sure to keep the door to the balcony open to allow a breeze to blow across his rooms.

He returned to the work of copying the scrolls on his table. The first one he picked up was the story of "The Two Brothers," which centered on one brother's wife who tried to seduce the other brother. This story always reminded him of David and the women who kept throwing themselves at him.

Thut-Moses felt like he had finally returned home. He enjoyed the sumptuous furnishings of Pharaoh's palace. He looked forward to hearing about the complicated intrigues in a court where the Pharoah already had thirty sons, from twenty different wives and concubines. He had lived in courtly surroundings for years. He knew that lesser wives were always plotting for ways to gain favor for their sons, to advance a son towards the throne. However, Rameses III was a man in seemingly excellent health who could expect a long life. Any succession battle was likely decades in the future.

Thut-Moses thought often about the King of Ugarit and his First Wife. He thought about David and his marital troubles as well. Thut-Moses knew that they were safe in their mountain retreat. He hoped the King was properly entertained by David and his songs; and had maintained his supply of honeyed red wine and cannabis.

When he finished the work of copying "The Tale of "Two Brothers," he put it aside and picked up a scroll from the wisdom literature: "The Words of Amenenope." Written over a hundred years ago and copied by scribes for the intervening three generations, it was a compendium of advice from a father to his son. Thut-Moses enjoyed the work of copying because it gave him time to ponder the personality behind the words.

He thought of Amenenope as a rather strict father. He himself had been taught this list of sayings while he was in training, in scribal school. The work offered an excellent introduction to how one should behave in a royal court: be respectful, be circumspect, and above all, avoid difficult characters.

One of his favorite sayings was: "Do not toil to gain wealth…wealth makes itself wings like geese and flies away into the heavens." When he read this bit of wisdom as a child, he did not understand it. As an adult, he understood it well. When he was taken captive by the Sea Peoples in Ugarit, that was certainly the flight of all sorts of luxuries and freedoms, not to mention decent food and a good bed to sleep on at night.

Or the saying about cherishing wisdom. "Do not waste your breath talking to a foolish man. It is a waste of breath." He had met his share of foolish men.

While he missed the Queen and the King and his friend David, he found he was happy to be back in Thebes, with access to the wisdom of his predecessors. Egypt had a three-thousand-year tradition of Pharaohs and of writing.

He missed the epics of Ugarit. The stories of their gods and their misbehavior or malice or arguments with each other were quite charming, he thought.

Here in Egypt, there was all that fuss about the Book of the Dead and preparation for the afterlife. He did not think that building tombs filled with magical incantations from the Book of the Dead was all that efficacious in expediting one's journey into the afterlife. He was happy enough in this iteration of life and grateful for the gifts he had been given, by whichever gods controlled such things.

He picked up his pen again and continued copying the words of wisdom from Amenenope. As his friend the Queen had said: nothing made him happier than perusing old manuscripts. He felt like he could travel back a century or millennium and see the world through the eyes of the ancients.

As the afternoon shadows grew long across the terrace, he took a break from his scribal duties. A woman attendant brought him some wine and something to eat. The woman was in her thirties; quite handsome, with olive skin, a long braid of black hair running down her back, and a linen sheath of good quality. She had a lovely smile. She gave him a plate of fruit and cheeses. She also provided a flask of wine.

"Sit down and share a cup of wine with me," Thut-Moses offered. "I know few people here in Egypt. I just met Pharoah and the elderly councilor at his side. It has been quite a day." She accepted a cup of wine and sat on a nearby chair.

"How did it go? I know the throne room, I know the councilor of whom you speak. He is a good man, a smart man."

"We spoke about the threat posed by the Sea Peoples. I spent eight weeks on one of their ships, as a captive. So I got to know them, unfortunately."

"In my village, in the Valley of the Kings, we heard little about the Sea Peoples," she said. "They came six years ago, no? I was married then, raising two children. I was busy and spent little energy on things outside the house."

"How long have you been working at the palace?" asked Thut-Moses.

"It's been three years now. My mother watches my children. I like the palace. There is always something going on. The gossip in the women's quarters is always excellent," she said.

Thut-Moses laughed. "I imagine so. What with twenty wives and I do not know how many children."

She went on to share some of the intrigue to which she was privy. He found her delightful. She was quick with words and had her own opinions about the goings-on in the court. She reminded him of Queen Donitaya in that regard.

As the shadows grew even longer across the balcony, she stood to her feet. "I must go. But thank you for the conversation," she said. She smiled a blazing smile, did a respectful bow and withdrew.

After she left, he thought, "I would enjoy further conversations and cups of wine with her." So much for intellectual solace among the writs of the ancients. He started looking forward to the more mundane comforts of good conversation with an attractive, witty woman.

EPILOGUE: THE COLLAPSE OF THE BRONZE AGE

U garit was destroyed around 1190 BC. In 1177 BC, the Egyptians fought a battle with the Sea Peoples and won. But they emerged from their triumph weaker than they had been before. Their treasuries were depleted. Their trade routes were interrupted by the mayhem wrought by the Sea Peoples and the general chaos of those times. The Egyptians were no longer able to sustain the powerful empire they had held for centuries.

Ugarit was not the only city that was razed and levels during these years. Scores of city states in the Aegean and the Near East, those that had been thriving for centuries in the brilliance of the Bronze Age civilization, came to an end. The Hittite empire also collapsed. Only recently, in roughly the last hundred years, have scholars become aware of the writings of the lost city of Ugarit and of other cities of the ancient Near East.

AUTHOR'S NOTE – October 2023

We just came through the COVID-19 pandemic. The pandemic inspired me to write a story about another time when destruction loomed over the known world. This little-known time was over 3,000 years ago when a complex, inter-related civilization collapsed.

They too were dependent on international trade. They too experienced the interruption of trade routes. And an existential crisis. Theirs was due to an invasion by enemy ships. Ours was due to an invasion by a deadly pandemic.

Our distress has so far been reversible. But the specters of climate change and wars and further pandemic and political discord still loom over our heads.

A story about how individuals deal with massive changes and forced migrations still seems apt, as does a story of how a sophisticated, multicultural civilization can thrive for hundreds of years and then collapse, disappearing from the annals of history.

"There is nothing new under the sun."—Ecclesiastes 1:9

SOURCES

Ugarit: Tales from a Lost City is a fictional narrative based on historical sources. The sequence of events leading to the attack on Ugarit by the Sea Peoples is as historical as possible, based on artifacts found in the ruins of the city,

Most poignant were the letters on clay tablets found in the ruins of the Palace, recording the last days of the city. Other tablets found in the temple compound provided the epics of El, Baal, and Anat.

In the writing of this book, another source proved invaluable: the Hebrew Bible. The Israelites entered the southern margin of Canaan around the time that Ugarit and other coastal cities fell. The newly-arrived Israelites would have understood the language spoken by their neighbors in the land. Hebrew is a cognate of Canaanite. They are both Western Semitic languages.

And Ugarit had been a part of Canaan. At its northmost margin, its language was Canaanite; its gods were from the Canaanite pantheon. The rhythms of its poetry, its metaphors for the might of its gods… these would have been accessible to the new arrivals in the land.

Modern-day scholars have identified stories and literary devices that are shared between Ugaritic literature and the stories in the Hebrew bible. Several stories in this book were inspired by Biblical passages.

Yet another source was Homer's Odyssey. The Trojan War likely took place before the fall of Ugarit. Homer's stories provide vivid descriptions of mores and military matters of the Late Bronze Age.

No one knows exactly where the Sea Peoples came from, but I adopted the theory that they came from the Baltics or Black Sea area. Mycenaeans and Cretans who were swept up in the general chaos of the time and took to sea raiding as a livelihood also likely joined the Sea Peoples.

These sources and others cited in the following section ("For Further Reading") have filled in the gaps of our knowledge of what life was like in the lost city of Ugarit, in a time before the stories of the Hebrew Bible and well before the time of the classical Greeks.

See UGARITTALES.com for detailed citations and notes.

****

Addendum

The Canaanite cities of Tyre, Byblos, and Sidon survived the Bronze Age Collapse. They picked up the trade routes that Ugarit had formerly controlled. This triad of city-states prospered and became known to the Greeks as "Phoenicians" -- which means "purple" in Greek, in honor of the purple dye they produced. Their trade empire spanned the length of the Mediterranean Sea, from its eastern shores all the way to Spain.

Along with trade goods, the Phoenicians brought with them a novel writing system--the "Phoenician alphabet." In this book, I propose it was invented by a scribe from Ugarit who spent time in Tyre. Historians agree it was someone who spoke a Semitic language; likely inspired by the phonetic system of letters used in Ugarit. Whoever invented the alphabet, it became a best-seller. It served as the basis for the Greek alphabet that the Homeric scribe used five hundred years later, to record the Odyssey and Iliad -- and eventually for the English alphabet that we use today.

FOR FURTHER READING:

• Berlin, A and Brettler, M.Z., The Jewish Study Bible. Oxford University Press: 2014.

• Cline, E. H., 1177 BC: The Year Civilization Collapsed. Princeton University Press: 2014

• Cline, E.H. , After 1177 BC: The Survival of Civilization. Princeton University Press, 2024.

• Coogan, M.D. and M.S. Smith, Stories from Ancient Canaan. Westminster John Knox Press: 2012

• Coogan, M.D., Ancient Near Eastern Texts. Oxford University Press: 2013.

• Craigie, PC, Ugarit and the Old Testament. Eerdmans Publishing Co.: 1983

• Drews, Robert. The End of the Bronze Age. Princeton University Press: 1993

• Holst, S. Phoenicians: Lebanon's Epic Heritage. Santorini Books 2021

• Master, D. "Piece by Piece: Exploring the Origins of the Philistines." In Biblical Archaeology Review, Volume 48, issue 1, page 30. Spring 2022.

• Pfeiffer, C.F. Ras Shamra and the Bible. Baker Book House: 1962

• Sandars, N.K. The Sea Peoples: Warriors of the Ancient Mediterranean. Thomas and Hudson 1978, revised 1985.

• Wachsmann, S. Seagoing Ships and Seamanship in the Bronze Age Levant. Chatham Publishing: 1998

• Wilson, E. The Odyssey, by Homer. Norton and Company:2018.

• Yon, M. The City of Ugarit at Tell Ras Shamra. Eisenbrauns Publishing: 2006

ABOUT THE AUTHOR

Janet Tamaren is a retired physician. She practiced in rural Kentucky for twenty years. She now lives in Denver with her husband. She has three children and two grandchildren. She enjoys writing and has written two books: a memoir about doctoring and a study guide to stories from the Hebrew Bible. She started writing this book about Ugarit during COVID lockdown. "This book is about another time and place where global trade networks came to a screeching halt, where a high-level civilization was threatened (and experienced) collapse. A time three thousand years ago: before the time of the Greeks and before the stories of the Hebrew Bible."

Follow Janet at www.historiumpress.com/janet-tamaren

or at www.jtamaren.wordpress.com

www.historiumpress.com

9 781964 700342